MACMILLAN READERS
UPPER LEVEL

CHITRA BANERJEE DIVAKARUNI

The Mistress of Spices

Retold by Anne Collins

Founding Editor: John Milne

The Macmillan Readers provide a choice of enjoyable reading materials for learners of English. The series is published at six levels – Starter, Beginner, Elementary, Pre-Intermediate, Intermediate and Upper.

Level control
Information, structure and vocabulary are controlled to suit the students' ability at each level.

The number of words at each level:

Starter	about 300 basic words
Beginner	about 600 basic words
Elementary	about 1100 basic words
Pre-Intermediate	about 1400 basic words
Intermediate	about 1600 basic words
Upper	about 2200 basic words

Vocabulary
Some difficult words and phrases in this book are important for understanding the story. Some of these words are explained in the story and some are shown in the pictures. From Pre-Intermediate level upwards, words are marked with a number like this: ...³. These words are explained in the Glossary at the end of the book.

Contents

A Note About The Author

Chitra Banerjee Divakaruni was born in 1956 in Calcutta, India. She is a poet and a writer, and has been a teacher. At the age of nineteen, Chitra left India and went to live in the United States. In America, she continued her studies in English and gained a Masters Degree at Wright State University in Dayton, Ohio. Later she gained a Doctorate (Ph.D.) from the University of California at Berkeley.

Chitra earned money for her education by doing many different jobs. She looked after children, she was an assistant in an Indian store, she worked in a bakery, and she cleaned instruments in a science laboratory. While she was at Berkeley, she served food in the dining hall to earn extra money to pay for her studies.

Chitra Divakaruni's writing has been published in more than 50 U.S. magazines, including *Atlantic Monthly* and *The New Yorker* and has been translated into 14 languages, including Dutch and Japanese. She has written three novels and several books of poetry. Many of her poems are about South Asian women's experiences of coming to live in America. For many years she has been interested in women's rights. In 1991 she helped to found Maitri, an organization in California which helps South Asian women who have been badly treated by their husbands or partners.

For 20 years Chitra Divakaruni lived in the San Francisco Bay Area and taught at Foothill College. In 1997, she moved with her husband and their two children to Texas where she now teaches creative writing at the University of Houston.

Collections of poems:
Dark Like the River (1987)
The Reason for Nasturtiums (1990)
Black Candle (1991)
Leaving Yuba City (1997)

Novels:
The Mistress of Spices (1997)
Sister of My Heart (1999)
The Vine of Desire (2002)

Collections of short stories:
Arranged Marriage (1995)
The Unknown Errors of
  Our Lives (2001)

Multitude (editor) (1993)
We, Too, Sing America
  (editor)

Sister of My Heart was made into an award-winning TV movie in India, in 2001.

A Note About This Story

This is a novel about magic, mystery and love. The story begins in a small village somewhere in India near the coast of the Indian Ocean and continues in Oakland, California in the United States.

Oakland is 4.5 miles east of San Francisco, which is one of the largest North American cities on the Pacific Ocean. A mixture of different races of people live there—white Americans, African-Americans, Asians from India and the Far East, and Latin Americans. The northern part of Oakland is connected to the Downtown district of San Francisco by the Oakland-San Francisco Bay Bridge which crosses the narrowest part of San Francisco Bay.

Beneath the surface of the Earth in this part of the world there are cracks—or faults—between the enormous plates of rock that cover the inner layers of the planet. The largest fault is the San Andreas Fault, which extends the full length of the state of California—about 600 miles—from the Gulf of California, north-west to Cape Mendocino. Each year these plates move about 1–1.6 inches when the hot, liquid rock deep within the Earth releases huge amounts of energy and pushes the plates against one another. If these movements are resisted then energy builds up and pushes large sections of the plates together violently. This energy creates earthquakes and causes a great amount of damage. Records of earthquakes have been kept in California since 1769 and they occur regularly. In 1906 a terrible fire caused by the biggest record-ed earthquake destroyed most of the city of San Francisco. There were also strong earthquakes in 1989 and 1994. In 1989, 62 people died and there was at least 6 billion[4] dollars' worth of damage to the southern area of San Francisco. Buildings and roads in California are built in a way that allows them to bend during an earthquake, but in 1994 the earthquake was so powerful that the raised section of the Santa Monica Freeway outside Los Angeles crashed down onto the highway called Interstate 5.

Tilo, the heroine of this story, has magical powers and she uses spices to help people who are in trouble. She believes that spices contain powerful magic and she uses them to help people who are lonely, sick, unhappy, or want to find love. Spices are substances made from plants and they are added to food to give it a particular flavor. They are also used as medicines. The food of South and South-East Asia is famous for its many different strong flavors which are created by spices. The most powerful and strongest spices come from plants that are grown in these countries. Spices have been bought and sold throughout the world for thousands of years. When they think of spices, people imagine the heat and strong sunlight of those countries, and the bright, exotic colors of the plants, flowers and people's clothes. Both Indian and English names for the spices are used in this story.

til (sesame). Sesame is a tall plant that grows in climates that are hot and wet. It has white seeds which are cooked until they are golden-brown. Tilo believes that sesame is an effective medicine for diseases of the heart and liver.

adrak (ginger root). Taken from the ground, the root of fresh ginger has a long, twisted shape and pale brown skin. Inside the skin, the flesh is golden-yellow in color. It has a very hot, sweet taste. In this story, ginger gives courage and strength.

haldi (turmeric). This bright yellow spice comes from a root which is dried and ground up into a powder. It gives a strong yellow color to everything it touches. For Tilo, turmeric is the spice of love and luck.

kalo jire (black cumin). There are two types of cumin plants—some have black seeds and others have white seeds. White cumin is used most commonly in cooking. The thin, long, light brown seeds have a flavor of lemon and pepper. *Kalo jire* is black cumin. These small black seeds are used for protection against evil.

dalchini (cinnamon). Cinnamon is the dried, rolled bark or skin of a tree that grows in southern India, the West Indies and Sri Lanka. The bark is ground into a red-brown powder or used whole, to flavor sweets and desserts. Cinnamon has a warm, sweet smell. It is the spice of friendship, or it can destroy enemies.

hing (asafetida). The liquid inside the stem of a plant that grows in Iran and Afghanistan is dried into a dark brown, sticky resin. It has a powerful, strong smell and is used in very small amounts to flavor stews and soups. Tilo says that asafetida is an antidote[2] to love. It prevents people falling in love and makes them strong in battle.

methi (fenugreek). This plant grows to a height of about 2 feet. It has dark green leaves which are eaten as a salad. The seed pods grow to 8 inches long and the seeds inside are yellow-brown and have a strong, sweet smell and bitter taste. They are ground into a powder to flavor pickles and chutneys. Pickles are vegetables and fruits that have been cooked in a mixture of oil, lemon or lime juice, and vinegar with salt, sugar, and spices. Pickles can be sweet or sour, mild or hot. Chutneys are made of fruit, vegetables, and spices that have been cooked together with sugar to make thick pastes. Pickles and chutneys are eaten with most meals in India.

kanwal (lotus root). Lotus plants grow in water. Their roots are crisp, long, and white, and taste like sweetened cream. Lotus root is eaten fresh, or cooked in sugared water to make sweets and desserts. Lotus is the spice of love.

makaradwaj (King of Spices). This magical spice makes people feel young and passionate[4]. It strengthens love.

badam (almond). A sweet white nut from a tree that grows in many parts of the world. Almonds are used in sweets and desserts.

kesar (saffron). Saffron comes from flower petals of the crocus plant. It is the most expensive spice in the world, because the petals are difficult to pick. Cooking rice with a few leaves of saffron gives it a yellow color and a warm, delicate flavor. Tilo mixes almond and saffron together. She says that when they are boiled in milk, people who drink the mixture will think sweet thoughts and say sweet words. They will forget their anger and their problems.

soonf (fennel). A tall plant which has soft, very narrow leaves, and large flat flowers with many seeds inside. The seeds have a sweet and warm flavor. Fennel strengthens the mind.

manjistha (Indian madder). A climbing plant that has very long roots. *Manjistha* makes people calm, and it takes away their anger.

kalo marich (black peppercorn). Peppercorn is one of the most important spices and is used throughout the world. The fruits of the pepper tree are green when they are growing. The tiny fruits become red when they are ripe and there is a small white seed inside. If the green fruits are stored in vinegar, they remain green in color. White peppercorn seeds become black when they are dried. *Kalo marich* makes people tell the truth and tell their secrets.

kantak (thorn-herb). This magical plant has sharp, very thin black thorns. Tilo uses it to make a mixture that can give a person powerful pains in their stomach. But when someone takes *kantak*, people will believe everything that person says and will obey that person.

lanka (red chillies). Chillies are the fruits of the chilli pepper plant which originally came from South America. Chillies can be used fresh or dried. Dried chillies are often ground into powder. Chillies are very hot and the seeds inside are particularly powerful. In this story, chillies are spices which can fight evil or cause destruction.

1

The Island of Spices

I am a Mistress of Spices. I know everything that there is to know about spices and their magical powers. I know where each spice comes from, and what its color means, and what its smell means. I know its deepest secrets.

The most powerful spices come from India, the land where I was born. India is a land of passionate poetry and glowing colors. If you stand in the center of my store and turn around slowly, you can see every kind of spice that has ever grown in India, here together on the shelves.

I was born in a village during a terrible thunderstorm. I was born with a caul[3] over my face, which caused the midwife[4] to cry out in fear and surprise.

My parents' faces were full of disappointment. They had been hoping for a boy, but I was a girl. A girl would bring them poverty, when they had to pay a dowry[1] to a husband.

Perhaps it was because of the strange circumstances of my birth, but from my earliest years I had unusual powers. I knew many secrets about the people in my village. I knew who stole the water-carrier's buffalo[1]. I knew which servant girl was sleeping with her master. I knew where gold was buried in the earth, and where a lost ring could be found. I warned the village headman about a flood, days before the water covered the land.

As time passed, my name became well known in the cities on the other side of the mountains. People heard about my strange powers and they came to our small house to ask for my help. Often these people brought me gifts that were so expensive that the villagers talked about them for days.

I cured the sick daughter of a powerful man. I foretold[3] the death of a wicked leader. I made good winds blow for sailors who were crossing the sea—I did this by drawing magical patterns on the ground. It was all so easy. I enjoyed the good things that my powers brought me, and I enjoyed the effects of my powers on the people around me.

Soon, I grew extremely proud and vain[2]. I sat on cushions made with gold thread. I ate from silver plates and wore clothes of the finest materials. I looked at myself in mirrors decorated with jewels and I admired the way I looked. At mealtimes I ate the best pieces of food and threw the rest on the floor for my brothers and sisters. My mother and father didn't show how angry they were because they were afraid of my powers and they loved the good life which my powers brought them.

When I saw the fear in my parents' eyes, I felt a great happiness. I, who had been one of the least important members of the family, had now become the most important member—I was famous. But I also felt a deep sorrow. I had wanted to win my parents' love, and I had only won their fear.

My fame continued to grow, but I was soon bored with my life. I longed[2] for something exciting to happen. And then something *did* happen—something more terrible than I could have imagined.

Sailors had taken stories about my powers across the seas. A gang of pirates[4] heard these stories and they decided to kidnap[4] me so that I would bring them luck.

One evening, when my family and I were eating our meal, the pirates arrived in our village. They burned all the other houses, then they broke through the bamboo walls of my father's house. They kicked over plates and jugs and scattered rice, fish, and honey everywhere.

One of the pirates plunged a sword into my father's heart, and the others attacked the women. They took carpets from the walls and they made a pile of jewelry on a skirt that one of my sisters had been wearing.

I tried to stop the pirates, but suddenly my magic powers were useless. The men seized me and carried me, a helpless prisoner, through the burning village. I heard the cries of terrified animals, and the screams of dying people. It was my fault that the pirates had destroyed[4] my village and killed my family, and as they carried me away, I prayed in my mind for forgiveness.

I lived with the pirates for more than a year, but I wasn't their prisoner for long. Soon after I was kidnapped, my powers returned to me and I grew stronger than the pirate chief. I became the chief myself—the queen of the pirates. During all that time, I felt terrible guilt[2] because of what had happened to my village and to my family. For a whole year, the guilt burned in my mind.

———

I can't remember now who first told me about the Island of Spices. But as soon as I heard about it, I knew that it was my destiny[3] to go there. The Island had existed since the beginning of time. I learned that a very powerful witch lived there—a woman who knew everything about spices. She was called the Old One and she taught girls how to use the magical powers of spices.

When I heard about the Island, I made the pirates sail our ship towards it. One evening, we saw it like a cloud on the horizon[4]. An hour later, we dropped the ship's anchor into the sea and stopped quite close to the Island. And that night, while the pirates slept, I dived into the dark ocean and swam to the shore. I dragged myself up onto the sand and fell into a deep sleep.

I will never forget the voice that woke me in the morning.

"What has the god of the sea thrown onto our shore today?"

I opened my eyes and looked up. The words had been spoken by a woman—old but very beautiful—who was surrounded by a group of young girls. Suddenly I realized that the sea had torn away my clothes and that I was naked. At that moment, the old woman took off her soft gray shawl[4] and put it around my shoulders. As she did so, I smelled a wonderful and mysterious smell of spices.

"Who are you, child?" the old woman asked. "What do you want here?"

I stared at her without speaking. The sound of her voice was as soft as the wind in the trees behind her. I knew that I wanted to stay near her forever. I felt a longing to be hers.

"Let me see your hands," she said.

She held my hands in hers. Her hands were soft, but at one time they must have passed through fire, because the skin had been burned and it was a pink-white color.

After a moment, she took a step back and let go of my hands.

"No!" she said.

I heard later that each year a thousand girls are sent away from the Island because they do not have the right hands. Their hands are the first things that the Old One examines when girls come to the Island, because it is a Mistress's hands which release the power from the spices.

But then the Old One took my hands in hers again, and examined the bones of my hands for a long time. She placed some spices in the centers of my palms.

"I should have made you leave that first day," the Old One told me much later. "Your hands were singing with danger. They were like a volcano[4] waiting to erupt. But I couldn't send you away."

"Why not?"

"Because the spices were singing too—they were singing in your hands."

2

Shampati's Fire

I became the Old One's cleverest pupil, quickly learning how to use the magical powers of the spices. But I was also the most arrogant[2] and impatient of her pupils. After some of us had been on the Island for a long time, the Old One—we all called her First Mother—told us some news. She told us that the time had come for us to leave the Island and follow our separate destinies.

"Daughters, it's time for you to become Mistresses of Spices and go out into the world," said the Old One. "Before you leave the Island, I will give each of you a new name. But you will have to give something in return. When you become Mistresses, your beautiful young bodies will change. They will become like the bodies of old women. Are you ready to accept that?"

Around me the other girls stood silently, shaking a little and looking down at the ground. It seemed to me that the prettiest ones looked at the ground the longest. But I looked at the Old One directly, without fear.

"Yes," I said. "We are ready."

"All right," said the Old One. She called us to her, one by one. Each of us knelt in front of her, and the Old One bent down and traced a new name on the young woman's forehead with her finger. But I didn't want the Old One to choose a name for me. I had already chosen my new name.

"First Mother, my name will be Tilottama," I told her. "People will call me Tilo."

"Tilottama—do you know what that name means?" she asked sharply.

But I had my answer ready.

"Yes, First Mother. The name comes from *til*."

Til is the golden-brown sesame seed.

14

"*Til* cures diseases of the heart and liver," I added.

The Old One laughed.

"Yes. But Tilottama was also the name of a girl—a beautiful dancer. She was the chief dancer at the palace of the Rain-god, Indra. Tilottama was perfect, a jewel among women. But you know what happened to her, don't you? She was warned[4] that she must never give her love to a man. But that proud, vain girl fell in love, and was sent away from Indra's palace. Her beautiful body became bent and twisted by a cruel disease. People turned away in disgust when they saw her."

"Yes, Mother," I said. "I know that. But I also know the rules that a Mistress must follow. I have made my vows[3]!"

The Old One sighed sadly and traced my new name on my forehead. I smelled the fragrance[4] of *til* seeds in the air, and I laughed at my success.

"I will not fall in love like Tilottama," I said.

My heart was full of love for the spices. I didn't need a man to love.

———

The Old One took us to a volcano on the Island—a sleeping volcano which hadn't erupted for many years.

"Mistresses, I have taught you all that I can," she said. "You must now decide where you want to go in the world."

She took some branches from a tree and waved them in the air around her. Soon the air was filled with a thick swirling mist. Then pictures started to appear in the mist, pictures of people in cities all over the world.

"Look," the Old One said. Then she started chanting[3] the names of the cities.

"Toronto, Calcutta, Rawalpindi, Kuala Lumpur, Dar-es-Salaam."

More pictures came, but now they showed ugly scenes. Clothes factories with tired workers. Crying women being pushed into police vans. Dirty streets with words of hate and cruelty written on the walls. Sad brown faces looking at us. We stared at them, silent with shock.

"London, Dhaka, Hasnapur, Bhopal, Bombay, Lagos."

We had always known that it would be hard to leave this beautiful place where we had lived for so long. But this was terrible. How could we leave our Island paradise[4] to go to the real human world with all its cruelty?

"Los Angeles, Jersey City, Hong Kong."

More and more pictures appeared. Then at last the Mistresses, their voices low and full of fear, began pointing at the different places.

"Perhaps I will go here, First Mother."

"First Mother, I am too frightened to choose. You must choose for me."

And the Old One gave to each Mistress the place which she had chosen. In this place, a Mistress would spend the rest of her life, using the power of spices to help people who needed help.

Soon, there were only a few places left, but still I said nothing.

Then suddenly I saw *my* place. First I saw beautiful pine trees and eucalyptus trees[4] and dry golden grass. I saw the houses of rich people, built on hillsides. But then the picture changed. And now I was looking at poor areas—dark apartment buildings in districts where dirty children chased each other through dark and dirty streets.

Even before the Old One said the name of the place, I knew it—Oakland. Oakland, California. And I knew too that this place was mine.

"Please think carefully, Tilo," said the Old One. "It would be better for you to choose somewhere else—perhaps a town in Africa."

"Oakland is the only place for me, First Mother."

"Go then," she said at last. "I cannot stop you."

I felt a wave[2] of joy rushing through me. I had gotten my wish.

That night, we built a pile of wood at the top of the volcano and made a great fire. Then we danced around it, singing about the legend of Shampati. Shampati was the bird who died in a fire, but then flew up out of the ashes to begin a new life. Now we were all going to be like Shampati—we were going to pass through fire to begin our new lives.

One by one, the Mistresses walked into the fire, and when they reached its center, they disappeared. When it was my turn, I closed my eyes, but I wasn't afraid. I believed what the Old One had told us. "You will not burn, you will not feel pain," she had said. "You will suddenly fall asleep. When you wake, you will have a new body. But it will feel as though[4] it has been yours forever."

I felt the Old One touch my arm.

"Tilo, my daughter," she said, "you are the cleverest girl and you are the one who has caused the most trouble. And you are the one that I love most. Tilo, before you begin your journey to America, here is something for you."

She placed a slice of *adrak*, ginger root, on my tongue, to give me courage. Then I stepped into Shampati's Fire. Tongues of flame licked my skin, then suddenly I slept.

When I awoke, I was lying on a floor and I was naked. I knew that I was in a store of some kind. I could see the store forming around me—a big room with many, many spices carefully arranged on its shelves. But I could still feel the powerful taste of the ginger root in my mouth.

Everything was silent. I lifted my arm and felt a scream rising in my throat. My hands were ugly and twisted, and I felt a sharp pain in my bones as I pushed myself up from the floor.

My beautiful hands were changed forever!

A wave of terrible sadness rushed through my body. And a wave of anger followed it. Yet the Old One had warned us that we would lose our beauty and wake with new bodies—the bodies of old women. There were no mirrors in the store, but I could see the shadow of my face in the grey glass of its large front window. I shut my eyes and moved away from it. It is a rule that, once a Mistress has received her magic Mistress-body, she must never again look at her reflection in a mirror.

After a while the anger went away. Perhaps the power of the spices helped me. For when I held them in my twisted old hands, the spices were singing more clearly than before. And suddenly I was truly happy.

3

The Spice Bazaar

My home now is this store in Oakland, California. The store has been here for only one year, but many people in this district think it has always been here. It looks old.

The store stands on the corner of Esperanza Street, between Rosa's Hotel and Lee Young's Sewing Machine and Vacuum Cleaner[4] Repair Store. Above my door are faded[4] brown letters which say: SPICE BAZAAR.

I, too, look as though I have always been here. When customers enter my store, they see an old, bent woman, with skin the color of sand, wearing a simple sari[1]. They see me standing behind a glass counter[4] that contains Indian sweets. And all the goods in the store remind my customers of India—the land most of them left behind when they came to America.

The customers don't know the truth about me, of course. They don't know that I'm not really old—that this body is not really mine. They don't see that my eyes are shining like fire. "Remember this," the Old One said, when she trained us on the Island. "*You* are not important. No Mistress is important. What is important is the store. And the spices."

The store has an inner room with no windows. Here I keep the rarest[4] spices, the ones which I gathered on the Island to use in times of special need. These are the spices which take away sadness and pain.

I have the power to use the spices, and I still have the powers that I was born with. I can see into the hearts and lives of all my customers. I know all their secrets. I know about all their problems.

———

Ahuja's wife is young. She is a regular customer at the store. She comes every week. But she buys only the most ordinary things— cheap rice or a small bottle of oil. Her name—Lalita—is as soft and beautiful as she is. But she doesn't think of herself as a beautiful person, she thinks of herself only as Ahuja's wife.

Lalita has said very little to me, but I know many things about her. I know that her husband drinks too much liquor. I know also that she has a great talent[4] for sewing.

Once I saw her looking at a beautiful sari in my store.

"Here," I said, taking it from its shelf and putting it around her shoulders. "This color looks so nice on you."

"No, no," she said quickly, turning towards me. "I was only looking at the embroidery[4]. I used to sew a lot. In India I went to sewing school. I had my own sewing machine, and many ladies asked me to make clothes for them."

"Wouldn't you like to work here in America too?" I asked.

"Oh, yes," she replied longingly. Then she looked at the floor. She can never tell me how lonely she is, or that her husband won't let her work. But I know how he shouts at her, and that sometimes he beats her, so that she has to wear sunglasses to cover the bruises on her face.

I decided to give her some *haldi*, turmeric, the spice of love and luck. If you rub it on your face, the silky yellow powder will give your skin a pale golden glow. Turmeric makes wrinkles[4] disappear, it takes away old age. So I secretly put a handful of turmeric, wrapped in paper, into her shopping bag when she wasn't looking. And I whispered some words of healing[3].

Haroun is another of my regular customers. He used to drive a big car—a Rolls Royce—for a rich Indian lady. The first time he came into my store he was with his employer. But later he came back alone and held out his hand to me.

"Lady, please tell my fortune[3]," he said. "Please read my palm."

"Your future looks good, very good," I told him, looking at his palm. "Great things will happen to you in this new land—this America. Riches and happiness, and maybe even love. When I look at your palm, I see a beautiful woman with dark eyes."

"Ah," he said with a little sigh. "Thank you, Lady." Before I could stop him, he bent to kiss my hands. I felt his soft warm lips against my skin, and a wave of pleasure ran through me. But at the same time something inside me twisted in fear, and I had a feeling of danger.

Three months later, Haroun has come to see me again.

"Lady, today I left my job with that rich woman," he tells me. "Last night I met an old friend—a friend from my village in India. He owns a couple of taxis and he's looking for a new driver. The pay is good, he told me, so I said yes. Lady, I must thank you. It's all because of the fortune you told me. Come and look at my taxi, it's just outside the store."

I know that I shouldn't leave the store. It is one of the Mistress rules. But I don't want to spoil Haroun's happiness, so I step through the door and onto the sidewalk. The taxi, as smooth and yellow as butter, is standing in the street. I put out my hand and touch it.

Suddenly a terrible vision of violence and pain comes into my mind. In my vision, I see the taxi with all its doors pulled open, and with someone bent over the steering wheel. I can't see who the person is.

"Are you OK, Lady?" asks Haroun. "Your face is very pale."

Suddenly, the vision vanishes.

"I'm fine, Haroun. It's a beautiful car. But please be careful in it."

"You worry too much, dear Lady. But if it makes you happy, give me a packet of magic spices next time I come. I'll put it in the car for luck."

He gets into the car and shuts the door. He starts the engine and drives off happily.

"You're imagining things!" I tell myself. "It will probably never happen."

But I can't stop thinking about Haroun. I must give him some *kalo jire*, black cumin, a blue black spice from the depths of the forests. It will help to protect him against evil.

———

Jagjit—a boy with a green turban[1]—comes to the store with his mother. He is ten-and-a-half years old, but he stands behind her, with his fingers touching her clothes.

"Oh, Jaggi, don't hold on to me like a girl," his mother says. "Go and get me a packet of *sabu papads*[1]."

Jagjit goes to the back of the store but he doesn't know what the *sabu papads* look like. I go to help him and find him staring at the shelves. He's confused. I hand him the *sabu papads* while his mother shouts at him from the front of the store.

"Why are you taking so long, Jaggi? Can't you see them? Is there something wrong with your eyes?"

I know that Jagjit has trouble in school because he knows only Punjabi, not English. In the schoolyard, the other kids bully[4] him. They pull his turban off his head and push him down on the ground so that his knees bleed. But Jagjit bites his lips and doesn't cry.

At home his mother is always angry with him.

"Jagjit, why are your school clothes always dirty?" she says. "Look, your shirt is torn. I can't buy you a new one. Do you think I'm made of money?"

At night Jagjit lies in bed with his eyes open, thinking of his village in India. He can't tell his mother that he's being bullied at school because she doesn't want to listen.

"Jaggi," she says, "what do you mean, you don't want to go to school? Your father is killing himself, working hard in the factory, so that we can send you to that school."

My heart[2] fills with sorrow for the boy. I want to help Jagjit so much. As his mother is paying for her things, I give him sweets flavoured with *dalchini*, cinnamon. Then I put more cinnamon in his turban without him noticing. Cinnamon—the warm brown spice of friendship that is also the spice which destroys enemies. It will give the boy strength that will grow in his arms and legs and mouth until one day he will shout "No!" Then the kids who bully him will leave him alone.

23

4

The Lonely American

One Friday evening, as I'm getting ready to close the store, a lonely American comes in.

It's not the first time I've seen an American man. Americans come into my store all the time. Usually I sell them what they want and forget about them. But sometimes I feel curious about them. For example, I often feel curious about Kwesi.

Kwesi is an African-American. His skin is as dark as wine, and his tightly-curled hair makes me think of clouds in the night sky. He walks like a graceful warrior, without sound, without fear. I long to ask him what work he does for a living, but I can't. The Mistress rules don't permit this kind of curiosity.

"Remember why you are going to America," the Old One told me before I went into the Fire. "You will be there to help your own people, and *only* them. If others need help, they must go somewhere else for it."

And so I don't look into Kwesi's heart to find out his secret desires. I weigh and pack the spices he buys. "That's very nice," I say when he tells me he's going to make *pakoras*[1] for a special friend, and then I wave goodbye to him. I keep the door[2] of my mind closed to him.

But this lonely man seems different from the other Americans who come here. I think I might have trouble closing my mind to *him*.

What is it that will make this difficult? It isn't the way he stands—relaxed and calm, with one hand in his pocket. It isn't his face, with its high cheekbones, his golden-brown skin, or his dark eyes. And it isn't his thick blue-black hair, the color of the feathers of a black bird's wings.

When other people come into the store, I always know at once what they want. But when this man comes, I *don't* know.

"I'm just looking at what you have here," he says when I ask him if I can help him. And he smiles at me, as though he's really seeing me—the real me inside this old woman's body. And it seems as though he likes what he sees. But how can that be?

I try to look into his mind, but I can't. He watches me as if he knows what I'm doing and is amused by it. No one has ever looked at me like that before. He is searching *my* mind.

I want to tell him that I am searching too. I had thought that all my searching was finished when I found out about my power over the spices. Now that I've seen this man, I'm no longer sure. But I hear a voice in my head.

"A Mistress must have no desires of her own," the voice says. "She must fill the loneliness in her heart with the needs of the people she serves."

So I tell the American, in a business-like voice, "You are welcome to look at my stock[4], but I must get ready to close the store for the day."

To give myself something to do, I start moving a bin[4] of rice to the other side of the doorway.

"Let me help you," he says.

Before I can stop him, he has put his hand on the edge of the bin, touching mine. The warmth of his hand goes through me like fire.

"You've got a great place here. I love everything about this store," says the American.

Then he moves away from me.

"I'm sorry, you need to close now," he says, and his voice has suddenly become formal[4]. He raises his hand in farewell. "I'll be seeing you."

After he leaves, I wander around the store, feeling dissatisfied, not wanting to lock up[4] yet. Outside, the streetlights come on. Men and women on their way home are going down into the subway. A thick yellow mist fills the empty streets, and in the distance I can hear the wail[4] of a siren—the sound of danger.

I am looking for a spice for the lonely American. But I can't find the right one. Nothing seems suitable. I can't stop thinking about the man's eyes, which are as dark and deep and dangerous as a tropical[4] night. And why do I think that he is lonely? Perhaps there is someone waiting for him at home—a beautiful woman with hair like golden thread. Suddenly, I remember the Old One's words again.

"If you let your own desires affect your thoughts," she said, "you will not see things clearly any more. You will become confused, and the spices will no longer obey you."

I go into the inner room and run my fingers along the dusty shelves. I close my eyes. I am going to trust my hands, not my eyes, to find the right spice for the lonely American.

After a few moments, my hands close around something hard with a bitter smell. I open my eyes and see that my fingers are holding a piece of *hing*, asafetida. Asafetida is the antidote to love. This is the spice that makes men strong in battle, hardens their hearts, and takes away all softness from them.

I drop the piece of asafetida into a small box, and on the box I write, FOR THE LONELY AMERICAN. Then I return to the main part of the store and I push the box to the back of the shelf under the cash register[4], where it will wait until the American comes back.

But later I look deep into my heart, and I know that I am not going to give the asafetida to the lonely American. I don't *want* to harden his heart against love.

———

The day after the lonely American first comes to my store is a Saturday. Usually I love Saturdays—they are my busiest days. I sometimes put up signs about special offers: FRESH METHI. DIWALI[1] SALE. LOWEST PRICES. VIDEOS OF THE LATEST INDIAN MOVIES.

27

But this Saturday I feel restless and impatient. The Indian radio station is playing a song about a beautiful girl with silver bracelets. There is a smell of the sea in the air which makes me long to open some windows. I can't concentrate on my work.

The lonely American is not among my Saturday customers and I am very disappointed. He promised to come again, I tell myself. Then I feel angry because he didn't really promise anything. Suddenly I'm tired of thinking about the needs of my customers. I want to think about my own needs.

I know how easy it would be to use my magic powers to make him come to me. All I would have to do would be to burn some *kanwal*, lotus root, in the evening, speak some magic words, and he wouldn't be able to keep away. Lotus root is the spice of love. And if I really wanted to attract the lonely American, I could do something so that he wouldn't see this old woman's body. I could use *makaradwaj*, the King of Spices, to make me young again.

"I worry about you, Tilo," the Old One told me the day I left the Island. We were standing on the highest part of the volcano. Far below us the waves crashed onto the shore, white and silent, like waves in a dream.

"I know your character," she went on. "You are brilliant, but you have a fault. You are like a diamond with a crack running through it. You may not be able to resist the temptations[4] that you will find in America."

"Mother, you don't have to worry about me," I told her. "Tonight I'm going to walk into Shampati's Fire. The Fire will burn away all desire."

She sighed. "I hope it does that for you," she said.

If the lonely American does come back to my store, it must be because of his own desire, not because of my magic powers.

5

Geeta's Grandfather

Every week, an old Bengali gentleman comes to my store to do his shopping. The old gentleman lives with his son, who is called Ramu, and Ramu's wife, Sheela, and their daughter, Geeta.

Geeta often comes to my store too. She's an attractive, intelligent girl and I like her very much. She worked very hard at college and now she has a good job with a big engineering company.

Geeta has grown up in America and she wants the freedom that American girls have. But for Geeta's grandfather, the traditional values[4] of Indian family life are very important. Because of this, there are many things about Geeta's behavior that he can't understand and doesn't approve of.

"She works late in the office," the old man tells me sadly. "There are men working there in the evenings too. Sometimes they bring her home in their cars, after dark. How will she ever get a husband if she behaves like that?"

"But this is America, not India," I tell him. "And even in India women are working in offices with men now."

But every week, Geeta's grandfather comes with more stories.

"Last Sunday, Geeta cut her hair so short that her neck shows," he tells me. "And when I told her that a woman's hair is the most precious thing she has, the silly girl just laughed and said, 'Oh, Grandpa, I needed a new style.' And she uses far too much make-up!"

Another time, the old man tells me that Geeta has bought a new car.

"It cost thousands of dollars," he says. "I told Ramu that the money should have been saved for her dowry. But he just said, 'It wasn't my money. She bought the car with the money that she earned at her job. Anyway, for Geeta, we'll find a nice Indian boy from Oakland who doesn't believe in giving dowries.' Ramu is my son, but sometimes I can't understand him!"

One morning Geeta's grandfather comes in without his shopping bag. I know that he doesn't want to buy anything but he stares at the things on the counter for a long time. Something is wrong.

"What do you need from me today?" I ask him gently.

As he answers, I can hear the fear in his voice.

"I've told Ramu a hundred times that he's not bringing Geeta up[4] in the right way. And now look at what's happened!"

"Well, what *has* happened?" I ask. I know I have to be patient and let him tell his story. My heart feels tight with fear, but I can't see into his mind.

"Yesterday, I got a letter from an old friend of mine in India. He told me that his family is looking for a wife for his grandson. The grandson is an excellent boy. He's only twenty-eight, but he's already an assistant judge. My friend asked me to send information about Geeta.

"I was very pleased, and as soon as Ramu came home, I told him the news. He *wasn't* so pleased. He said that Geeta had grown up in America and he didn't know if she would like living in a big family in India. We talked about it for a long time and at last Ramu said that we would tell Geeta about the boy."

I wait for the old man to continue his story.

"Well, last night, Geeta came in late as usual," he goes on, after a few moments. "She said that she'd gone to a pizza restaurant with some of her friends from work. Her father told her about the letter, and she started to laugh. 'Dad, are you serious?' she asked. 'Please tell me that you're joking. Can you really imagine me sitting all day in a hot kitchen in India, with a bunch of keys tied to the end of my sari?' That's what she said! Can you believe that?"

I don't reply so he goes on again.

"Her father didn't answer her, so I said, 'What's wrong with that, Geeta?' And Geeta said, 'I'm sorry, Grandpa, but an arranged marriage isn't for me. I'll choose my own husband. And actually, I've already found someone that I love.' Ramu and Sheela were very shocked. Sheela asked her, 'Who is it? What is his job?' and 'Do we know him?' "

The old man is finding this very difficult. Suddenly, he looks so sad.

"Geeta's face went very red," he continues. "She knew that she was making her parents unhappy. 'He works at the engineering company. He's a manager there,' she told us. 'His name is Juan— Juan Cordero.' As she said the name, I could see the shock on her mother's face."

The old man pauses for a moment. Then he tells me, "Well, *I* was shocked too. 'She's marrying a white man,' I said to Ramu. 'Dad, Mom, please don't be upset,' Geeta went on. 'Juan is a very nice man, you'll see that when you meet him. And he's not white, Grandpa, he's a *Chicano*[4]. His family came here from Mexico.' "

The old man looks at me, wanting *me* to be shocked. But he continues with his story.

"I told Geeta, 'You are going to bring shame on our family by marrying a man whose people are criminals and illegal immigrants[4].' Sheela was crying. 'Is this how you thank us for giving you so much freedom?' she asked."

He stops again. I know that soon he's going to ask me to do something. But he still has something to tell me.

"I told my son, 'Ramu I don't want to stay in this house any more. I want you to put me on a plane to India tomorrow. I'd rather die alone there than stay here in this country which I don't understand.' But Ramu wouldn't speak. Geeta looked at her father. 'Dad,' she said, shaking Ramu's arm. 'Please say something.'

"Ramu pulled his arm away as if he had had an electric shock. Then at last he did speak. 'Daughter, I trusted you,' he said, in a terrible voice. And Sheela and Geeta started shouting at each other. 'Go to your room! I don't want to see your face again!' Sheela told Geeta. 'You won't have to see it again. I'm leaving! And I'm never coming back!' said Geeta. 'I'll go and live with Juan. He's been asking me to do that for a long time.' She said that to her own father!" the old man told me sadly.

"Then Geeta went out and slammed the door behind her, and a moment later I heard the sound of a car engine starting. I closed my eyes. When I opened them again, I was alone. I went to my room, but all night long I couldn't sleep. This morning I left the house before anyone was awake and came straight to your store."

"But what can I do for you?" I ask the old man.

"I know you can help us," he says. "Many people talk about your powers. *Please* help us."

Geeta's grandfather looks down at the floor. He is not used to asking for help.

I quickly prepare a special mixture of *badam* and *kesar*, almond and saffron, to boil in milk.

"The whole family must drink some of this at bedtime," I say. "It will sweeten your words and thoughts. It will make you remember love, not anger. But I don't think I can solve your problems completely with this mixture. For the medicine to work properly, Geeta must come to see me herself."

"But she won't do that," says her grandfather hopelessly. He is silent for a time. "She won't come here," he says at last. "But perhaps you could go to her? I could show you where she works."

"That's impossible," I tell him. "It isn't permitted."

He says nothing more, but he looks at me with eyes like the

eyes of an animal in pain. And suddenly, for no reason at all, I think of my lonely American. Perhaps I too am like Geeta. I'm learning how love can twist itself around your heart like a rope, and pull you away from everything that you know is right.

"All right," I tell Geeta's grandfather. "I'll visit her—just this one time."

————

That night I dream of the Island. I have dreamed of it often, but this time the dream is different from all the others. The air is black and filled with smoke, and I can't see the sky or the sea clearly. The Island floats in a empty black hole. But I look closer and see that I am sitting under a fig tree with the other Mistresses. The Old One is asking us questions. We already know the answers.

"What is the first duty of a Mistress?"

"To help everyone who comes to her with problems."

"How must she feel towards those who come to her?"

"She must love everyone equally, and no one specially."

"Now, Tilo," says the Old One, "you are always too confident, so you are the best person to answer this next question. What happens when a Mistress breaks the rules and seeks her own pleasure instead of helping others?"

"Shampati's Fire—" I start to say, but the Old One interrupts me.

"I will tell you." Then, in the dream, she turns her face towards me, and I see something terrible. She has no nose, or eyes, or cheeks or lips. There is only a black hole where her mouth should be.

"When a Mistress uses her power for herself, when she breaks the rules—" she begins in a loud, ugly voice.

The black mouth stretches into a terrible smile. The Island begins to shake, the ground grows hot. I hear the roaring of the volcano. It is the most terrifying sound I have ever heard.

And then I wake up. But a voice in my head tells me what the Old One was going to say.

"When a Mistress gives her love to someone who she should *not* love, then *all* the people who she loves will be destroyed."

33

6

Spice Magic

Ahuja's wife, Lalita, hasn't been to the store for months, and I have been worried about her. Then one morning she comes to see me.

"I'm so unhappy, I don't know what to do," Lalita says.

She stretches out her hand and I hold it tightly. I take her into the little kitchen at the back of the store and we sit down at the table. I know that what I'm doing is against the Mistress rules, but I must try and stop her pain.

"My husband is very cruel to me," she says. "He doesn't allow me any freedom. He won't let me go out or talk on the phone. I have to tell him about every cent I spend. He reads my letters before I mail them. And he calls me on the phone all the time, to check on what I'm doing.

"He forces me to make love with him, and if I won't, he beats me. I used to be afraid of death, but not any more. Now I think about killing myself."

I can't see which spice will help her. And this is just what the Old One warned me about. I've become too worried about Lalita, so now I can't help her. I close my eyes and concentrate, until a spice name comes to me—*soonf*, fennel.

"I'll give you some fennel," I tell her. "It will strengthen your mind."

Lalita looks at me with despair in her eyes and stands up.

"I have to get home," she says.

I can see that she is disappointed that I am not doing more to help her. She doesn't believe that a spice will solve her problems. She is regretting that she has told me so many things about herself.

I look for some fennel to put into her hand. But I can't find it. I look around the store desperately. Suddenly I see some packets of the spice on top of a pile of *India Current* magazines. How did the fennel get there? I pick up a packet, and a copy of the magazine.

"Eat some of the fennel seeds every day, and read this magazine too. It might help you to stop thinking about your problems. And remember this—no man, whether he is your husband or not, has the right to beat you. And no man has the right to force you to make love. These things are not allowed!"

———

It is evening. I am sitting at the counter chopping *kalo jire* seeds with a sharp knife. I am making up a special spice packet for Haroun, to protect him.

I am concentrating, so I don't hear the lonely American come into the store. When I suddenly realize that there's someone with me. I look up quickly, and the knife cuts my finger.

"You're bleeding," the American says. "I'm sorry that I frightened you. I should have knocked on the door."

"It's OK," I tell him. "It isn't a deep cut, it's just a scratch."

I feel only happiness at seeing him again. The blood is dripping from my finger onto the pile of *kalo jire*, which is now red-black and ruined.

"Why did you come back?" I ask him.

"Perhaps you can read the reason in my hand," he says.

I place my fingers on his wrist. His golden-brown skin smells of lemon and salt. The smell makes me think of the hot sun beating down[4] on white sand.

Suddenly there is the sound of angry shouting.

"Lady! Lady! What's going on?"

It's Haroun. He has run into the store and he is looking suspiciously[4] at us. I snatch my hand back from the American. I feel like a young girl who has been seen by her father talking to a strange boy.

The American has walked away from me and he is wandering around the store, looking at the things on the shelves. Haroun watches him.

"Dear Lady," Haroun says to me quietly. "You must be more careful about who you let into your store. There are all kinds of bad people in this neighborhood[4]."

I am embarrassed because I am sure that the American can hear him.

"Lady, he's wearing expensive clothes, but that doesn't mean you can trust him," Haroun goes on, pointing at the American.

"Haroun, I'm not a child. I can take care of myself," I answer angrily. "Please don't insult my customers."

Haroun's face turns red. When he speaks, his voice is cold. I have hurt his feelings[2].

"I said those things because I was worried about you. But I'm only a poor taxi driver and I shouldn't give you advice. I don't have any right to tell you what to do. Goodbye."

He bows[4] to me formally and goes out into the night. The door closes behind him before I can say anything. I see the red-black *kalo jire* spilled on the counter like a dark stain.

"Sometimes I have an ache in my heart," the American tells me. "Here." He takes my hand and holds it against his chest.

"Your heart feels fine," I tell him.

"Yes, that's what all the doctors say."

His eyes are laughing at me. His hair gleams like a black bird's wing with the sun shining on it.

I know I should give him the asafetida, the antidote to love. I know I should send him out of my life forever. I start to reach towards the little box under the cash register—but then I stop. I don't want to give it to him. I want more time, just a little more time.

The next day, Kwesi, the handsome young African-American, comes into the store with a cardboard tube under his arm.

"Would you mind if I put a notice up in your window?" he asks.

Indian people put notices in my window all the time. They advertise parties, or businesses. But Kwesi isn't an Indian.

He pulls a poster from the tube and lays it carefully on the counter. I see a gold and black picture of a man with his fists raised for fighting and one leg stretched out in a powerful kick. Underneath the picture are the words, KWESI'S ONE WORLD DOJO[4], then an address.

"So you run a martial arts center," I say smiling. "I knew you were some kind of warrior. You're welcome to put your poster up here. But I'm not sure how many of my customers will be interested in martial arts."

We look around the store. Two middle-aged women in saris are looking at jars of pickles. An elderly man is looking at some small bottles of oil. He wants to buy the oil to cure his cough.

Kwesi smiles. "I'll find another place for the poster," he says.

I give him a packet of my best tea as a present, and walk with him to the door. "Come again, any time. Good luck with your dojo and with your life."

———

One morning, a teenage boy comes into the store with his mother's shopping list. His hair stands up stiffly, like the bristles of a brush. He is looking at goods on the shelves and at first, I don't recognize him. Then I look again and see that it is Jagjit.

"Jagjit, how are you?" I call to him.

He turns around angrily, ready for a fight. Then he sees me.

"How do you know my name?"

"You came here with your mother three or four times, maybe two years ago."

He shrugs[4] his shoulders and turns away from me. He doesn't remember. To Jagjit, I'm just another old woman like his grand-mothers, his aunts or his mother.

"Are things better for you at school now?" I ask him.

He turns again and stares at me angrily. "Who told you about things at school?"

I don't reply, and the expression on his face changes. "Yes, school is cool[4] now."

"And the other boys— you don't get any trouble from them?"

He smiles. "Nobody makes trouble for me any more. I've got good friends now—they're cool too."

I look into his eyes and I see pictures in them. I see pictures of boys in dark blue satin jackets and hundred-dollar boots. Boys wearing gold chains and bracelets. Boys with diamond rings on their fingers. Most of them aren't Indian boys.

"Yes, my friends look after me," Jagjit is saying inside his head. "They're only sixteen and already they're driving fast cars. These boys stood in the schoolyard watching my classmates bullying me, until one day they came over and told the bullies to go away. And since then I've never had any trouble. My friends bought me clothes, shoes, food, watches, computer games. And they taught me how to fight. They showed me how to use my elbows, knees, fists, boots, keys—and yes, a knife.

"And what did they want from me?" Jagjit continues in his head. "Not much! Sometimes they asked me to take a little box somewhere, or to keep a packet in my locker[4] for a day. When I'm older, maybe when I'm fourteen, I'll be with them all the time. I'll wear the same kind of jacket, carry the same kind of knife. And one day they'll give me a gun."

I hear the voice in Jagjit's head and suddenly I can't breathe. What have I done? Two years ago, I gave Jagjit cinnamon to give him strength against the bullies. But I never intended him to get mixed up[4] with a dangerous gang who will one day lead him into serious trouble.

Jagjit turns away again. He moves towards the door.

"Wait a moment," I say to him. "I want to give you something. It will make you even stronger and even more clever."

"I don't use those Indian medicines any more," he says. "I don't believe they work."

I look into his mind and I hear the name that his mother called him when he was very young. When I call him by this name his body shakes for a moment. He is remembering how his mother cared for him, and for a moment he wants to be a little boy again.

"OK," he says. "I'll take it to make you happy. But be quick. There's someone waiting for me outside."

I go to the little room where the rarest spices are kept and I fill a bottle with some medicine made from *manjistha*, Indian madder. This is the spice to make people calm, to take away their anger. I say some secret words over the bottle. Then I hurry back to the front part of the store, where Jagjit is waiting and I give him the medicine.

Jagjit leaves the store, and a moment later I hear the roar of a motorcycle engine. I cover my aching head with my hands, asking myself what went wrong. Why has Jagjit gotten mixed up with this gang? Is it his parents' fault? Or is it my fault? Did the spices want to punish me because I broke the Mistress rules?

7

Out Into the World

Geeta's grandfather has come into the store again. He hasn't mentioned Geeta, but I know he is wondering if I have been to visit her.

So this evening I prepare myself for my first adventure in America. I have never been away from the store before and I am a little frightened. So I boil a root of ginger in water. Ginger is the spice of courage. I pour the honey-colored liquid into a cup and drink it. It is so hot that it makes me cough. But I feel better now, stronger. I am ready to go to Geeta.

When I came to America, I was given no clothes for outdoor wear, just some old saris to wear in the store. So now I am going to have to buy some new clothes.

Outside, the rain is cold, and stings like needles as I lock the store door. I breathe the cold, wet air, then walk resolutely[4] down the empty street. At last I come to a big store. The name "Sears" is written on the windows and the doors. I turn towards the first door and it opens automatically for me, like the entrance to a magic land. I walk through the door and find myself in a huge, wonderful place.

Sears is very different from my spice store. There are so many things for sale—cosmetics, silver plates, thin silk nightdresses, things for the kitchen, video games from Japan. A whole wall of TV sets is talking to me.

I buy some cheap clothes to wear for my visit to Geeta. I also buy a large mirror, although I know that it is forbidden for a Mistress to look at her reflection. But I buy the mirror anyway, and ask the assistant if it can be delivered to my store later.

I go into a public rest room[4] in the store and put on my new clothes—some ordinary pants, a plain top, a brown coat, and a pair of strong brown shoes.

Outside the Sears store there is a bus stop with a line of people waiting at it. Nobody notices me. I am just one of the crowd. When the bus arrives, I get on it with everybody else.

Geeta's grandfather has told me where she works. The offices of the engineering company are in a tall building. It's like a tower of black glass with rows of shining windows. I go inside and ask the receptionist if I can see Geeta. She stares disapprovingly at my cheap clothes.

"Do you have an appointment?" she asks suspiciously. "No? Then I'm afraid I can't help you." She turns back to the keyboard of her computer. But I haven't come all this way just to be sent home again. I move closer to her. In a moment, I am standing beside her. She stops working and looks up at me.

"You *must* tell Geeta that I am here," I say. "It's very important."

I know that the receptionist is wondering if she should call for the security guard. But finally she presses a button on a machine at her desk, picks up a phone, and speaks into it.

"Geeta, there's a woman here to see you. Yes, I think she's Indian. No, she didn't tell me her name. OK, if you're sure." Then the receptionist turns to me and points to a door on the left side of the hallway.

"The elevator[4] is over there," she says. "Geeta Banerjee's office is on the fourth floor."

Geeta's office is a tiny room, without windows. She is sitting behind a metal table covered with cardboard files full of papers. I guess she is trying to write a report of some kind. When she sees me her eyes grow dull with disappointment. I wonder if she was expecting her mother instead of me.

"Please sit down," she says finally. "This is a surprise. You look different today. Did someone ask you to come and see me?"

"Yes."

"Was it Dad?" she asks in a voice that is suddenly full of hope.

"It was your grandfather, actually."

"Oh, him," Geeta says, and I can hear the hate in her voice. I know that she is thinking, "It's all *his* fault. He's the one who turned my parents against[2] me."

"Your grandfather loves you a lot," I say.

"He loves me? Hah! He doesn't know what the word love means. But he understands the word control! He wants to control my parents. He wants to control me. And whenever he doesn't get his way, he says 'Ramu, send me back to India. It's better if I die alone there.' He makes me so angry!"

She stops, and I am silent too, wondering what I can say.

"What did he think *you* could do to help?" she asks, staring at me.

"Nothing really," I say. "But now I've seen you, so I can tell your family that you're well."

"I don't know about that," she says. "I take sleeping pills every night, and still I can't sleep. Diana's been really worried."

"Diana?"

"Oh, I didn't go to live with Juan. I knew it would really upset Mom and Dad. So I called my friend Diana and asked if I could stay with her."

"Geeta," I say, "you're a very intelligent girl. It's very good that you didn't move in with Juan."

She tries to hide her smile, but I can tell that she is pleased. "Would you like to see Juan's photo?" she asks. She shows me a picture of herself together with a handsome young man with dark hair. He looks serious and also kind and gentle.

"He's very clever," she says, smiling. "He's from a very poor family, but he worked hard and got a scholarship[4] to college. If Dad could just talk to him, he'd see how wonderful Juan is."

"I'd like to meet him. Maybe you'll bring him to my store?"

"Sure. He'd like that. He's very interested in Indian culture and especially our food. You know, Mexicans cook with a lot of the same spices that we—"

Suddenly she stops, and looks straight at me.

"Now I remember. Grandpa once said that you know magic spells. That's why he's asked you to come and see me. Well, Grandpa is right *sometimes*! Thank you very much for coming—I feel much better now."

She comes downstairs with me, and pushes the photo of herself and Juan into my hand.

"Maybe you could tell my family that Juan and I aren't living together?" She kisses me on the cheek and her lips feel like a warm rose against my skin. "And here's my phone number, in case—well, in case," she adds. She gives me a card.

As she speaks, I'm making a plan in my head. I'll give the photo and her phone number to her grandfather when he next comes to my store.

———

Later, I fall asleep in the store, and when I wake up, the Old One is sitting by my head. I start to move away from her, fearing her anger. But on her face there is no anger, only a deep sadness.

"First Mother," I say softly. I hold out my hand to her, but there is nothing to touch. Her body isn't real—she is traveling in the spirit[3]. I remember how she used to make these journeys, and how she was always exhausted on her return from them.

"First Mother, is what I have done so very wrong?"

"Tilo, you should not have gone to see Geeta," she says.

"But, how else could I have helped her?"

"If you give help to anyone outside the protection of the walls of this store, your power will turn against you. Listen, Tilo! Mistresses have no real power of their own. It is the spices which have the real power. If you dream of love, you will make the spices hate you. Don't let the temptations of America lead you from your true path."

"You know all about my feelings?" I whisper. She doesn't answer. Already she is fading from the room.

"Mother, since you know the secrets of my heart, answer this question. What if a Mistress wants her life back? What will the spices—"

But she has gone. Only the spices are left, their dark power stronger than ever.

———

The next morning, two men knock hard on the door of my store.

"Delivery!" one of them shouts.

They are delivering the mirror which I bought at Sears. When the men have gone, I take the big mirror out of its box.

"Why are Mistresses not allowed to look at themselves?" I wonder.

I hang the mirror on the wall. The sunlight flashes on it, so I cover it with a cloth. I do not want to break the rules and look at my reflection in the glass today. I am not yet ready to discover more secrets about myself.

8

Raven's Story

It's a Monday when the lonely American comes to the store again. On Mondays the store is closed. Monday is my day of silence, when I go to the inner room and think about the Island. I can always see it in my mind—the coconut palms swaying, the soft sun seeming to float on the evening sea. I can smell the fragrance of wild flowers in the sweet heavy air, and I can hear the thin cries of the sea birds as they dive for fish.

But on *this* Monday, before I can go to the inner room, I see the lonely American standing outside the store, looking at the CLOSED sign. He is going to turn away, but I hurry to the door.

"Come in," I say. I am very happy to see him.

He steps into the store and starts to look at the different packets of spice snacks[1].

"I want to try one of these," he says, picking up a packet on which is written LIJJAT SNACKS—VERY HOT!!!

"Are you sure?" I ask doubtfully.

"Yes, absolutely."

I smile, remembering how I used to be on the Island. I was exactly the same as this man—so very sure that I knew exactly what I wanted.

"All right. But I warn you, the main spice in that snack is *kalo marich*, peppercorn. Peppercorn makes a person tell all their secrets."

"So, do you think I have secrets?" he asks. He takes some of the spice from the packet and puts it into his mouth. His strong white teeth bite into the snack.

"Mmm, it's great," he says. But I see that he is sucking air into his mouth, trying to cool his burning tongue.

"That snack is too hot for a white man's tongue," I say. "Maybe I should get you a cup of water."

"That would spoil the taste," he says. He sucks in some more air, but now he is thinking about something else. "So you think I'm a white man?"

"You look as if you are. I don't mean to insult you."

He smiles at me, but I can see he is still thinking.

"If you tell me your name," I say, "I'll *know* what you are."

The American finishes the snack in silence, but he shakes his head when I offer him more. I wonder if my question was too personal[4].

46

He stands up, goes to the door and opens it.

This is wrong! The peppercorn should be making him want to talk to me, to tell me his secrets. I don't want him to go. He doesn't have to say anything if he doesn't want to. I just want him to stay with me for a while.

He waits, his hand on the door, as if he's deciding what to do. Then suddenly, with an angry movement, he shuts the door again.

"What name shall I tell you? I've had so many."

———

Then the American begins his story.

"I'm not surprised that you thought I was a white man," he says. "For many years, I believed it too. I grew up in a house with a kind father, and a mother who I thought was the most beautiful woman in the world. But one day I discovered that my mother had a secret.

"When I was about ten, a strange man came to our house. He wore an old coat, torn under one arm, and jeans that smelled of animals. His boots were covered with dirt and his hair, which was straight and black, grew down to his shoulders. When Mother opened the door and saw him, her face suddenly went pale. She tried to close the door again, but the man pushed it open and came into the house.

"She sent me to wait in another room, but I could hear parts of her conversation with the stranger. 'Why do you come here to destroy my life?' she asked him in a hard voice. 'You ought to be ashamed, Evvie,' the man replied. 'You left your own people to live like the white people. You think that you're so fine and grand, but your little boy doesn't know who he really is. And now your grandfather is dying. That's what I came to tell you. Now do what you like.' When I heard the man's words, I was scared.

"Later, I went into the kitchen, hoping that my mother would explain to me who the strange man was. But she didn't say anything.

"The next morning, after Dad had gone to work, she put on her best clothes. 'Come on,' she said to me, 'we're going somewhere.' We got into her car and she drove a long way out of town. At last we turned into a narrow street with very poor houses, and wrecked cars in the yards. There were weeds and garbage[4] everywhere.

"She stopped the car and got out. Looking very proud, and holding my hand very tightly, she led me into a small house that smelled of wet clothes. It was full of dirty men and women with straight black hair, some of them drinking out of brown bottles. They weren't white people—they were Native Americans.

"On a bed in a corner of a dark narrow room I saw a thin shape under a blanket. I realized that it was an old man and that he was very ill. When he saw us, he raised his head. 'Evvie,' he said to my mother. Then he looked at me. 'Evvie's son...' he said. I understood that these people were my mother's people—my people."

The American breathes deeply and shakes his head.

"I can't believe I'm telling you all this garbage about my past," he says. "This peppercorn stuff must be very powerful."

"Your story isn't garbage," I say. But I know that he isn't going to tell me any more today, and that I will have to wait for the rest of his story.

"Anytime you want to talk," I say, "my door will be open for you."

His eyes are looking into mine and I wonder what he sees when he looks at me. Does he see an old woman, or does he see something else?

"Do you still want to know my name?" he asks.

"Yes," I say. "But only if you want to tell me."

"Well," he says shyly[4], "my name is Raven."

"But that's a beautiful name," I say. I think of those beautiful black birds which are called, in English, ravens. "It's the right name for you," I add.

I'm not impatient to know how he got his name. I know that there are many untold stories between us—his stories and mine.

"Raven, now I'll tell you my name. You are the only man in America—in the whole world—to know it."

He holds out his golden-brown hand to me. I touch it gently and I tell him my name.

49

9

Protection

The next day passes very slowly. A few customers come into the store and wander lazily around the shelves. They look at the goods, but they don't buy anything. I'm feeling very tired and it's hard for me to concentrate on them.

Then Kwesi comes into the store, and suddenly I feel better. I always feel happy when I watch Kwesi shopping because he chooses everything so carefully.

"I want to cook something special for my girlfriend," he says, smiling.

Kwesi is a happy person. If only I could make everyone who comes to me so happy, I would feel more successful. But the truth is that Kwesi was happy when he first came to me. I am not doing well with the people who are in real need of my help.

"Do you remember how you once wanted to put up a poster about your dojo, here in the store?" I ask. "I've been thinking about that. It's not a bad idea. You never know who might be interested. Do you have a poster in your car?"

He does. He brings the poster in and I help him fix it up next to the door. It looks very attractive, with its black and gold picture. I know that Kwesi is a tough man, but I also know that he is very kind. He really wants to help young people to protect themselves.

After Kwesi leaves, Geeta's grandfather comes in.

"I am having no luck with what you told me to do," he says. "I tried to talk to Ramu at dinner. I said that maybe we had been too hasty[4] and I asked him to call Geeta. I gave him her phone number and told him I had gotten it from some friends. But in a hard voice, a voice like stone, he refused even to think about the idea."

"Did you tell him that Geeta is staying with her girlfriend and not with Juan?"

"Yes. But he didn't want to hear anything about Geeta. He said, 'Why have you changed your mind now, Father—you, who disapproved of her behavior so strongly? I've listened to you enough already. When my daughter walked out of this house, slamming the door behind her, she walked out of my life.'

"All night long I couldn't sleep," the old man went on. "At midnight I got out of bed and went downstairs. I left the photo of Geeta and her boyfriend on the small table where Ramu sits and drinks his tea every morning. But when I came in later, after he had gone to work, I saw the photo lying on the floor."

I go to the inner room of the store, wondering what to do. Then I have an idea.

I search the shelves until I find a special spice, *kantak*, the thorn-herb. The plant has sharp, hair-thin, black thorns. You must not use too much *kantak* in a medicine. It is quite poisonous, and if you use too much, it can kill you. So I carefully break off just three of the hairs, cut them up and mix them with some honey. I fill a small bottle with the mixture. Then I go back into the store and hand the bottle to Geeta's grandfather.

"You said you would do anything for Geeta, to bring her back into the family," I say to him. "Then take this, and mix it into your rice at dinner time. It will give you very bad stomach pains, maybe for several days. But for one hour you will have the Golden Tongue. This means that whatever you say during that time, people will believe you. Whatever you tell them to do, they will obey you."

"I am willing to suffer the worst pains," says Geeta's grandfather very quietly.

I wait until it is evening and all the customers have left the store. Moths float around the light above the door and I can hear the soft sounds of their bodies hitting the glass. There has been a cold fear in my heart all afternoon—a fear that I can't hide any longer. It's a fear about Haroun.

I need to help him, but I upset him and I'm afraid that Haroun will not come to the store again. So how can I help him? Suddenly, the answer comes into my mind, so quickly that it surprises me. The answer shows me that I am no longer the Tilo who left the Island.

"If he won't come to you, you must go to *him*," says a voice in my head. "Yes, you must go out into America again. You cannot let Haroun be destroyed. You must take him some *kalo jire* for protection."

But now I have another problem—I must find Haroun but I don't know his address. Suddenly I remember that there are phones. I have never used a phone myself, but I know what phones are for. I must find a phone booth and call Haroun. I must call Geeta too. I have the card with her number, the card she gave me when I visited her.

I open the door and go out into the street. I find a phone booth and I make the call to Geeta first. The call is answered and I hear Geeta's voice, but it isn't really her speaking, I know that. I'm listening to an answering machine. I leave a message for her, asking her to come to the store alone, the day after tomorrow, at seven o'clock in the evening.

Then it's time to call Haroun. I don't know his number or where he lives, so I look in the phone book for his name. It isn't there.

Then I remember that Haroun has a friend—a man who I helped a long time ago. I find this man's name in the phone book and I call *his* number.

A woman answers the phone.

"I'm trying to find Haroun," I tell her. "Do you know where I can find him?"

At first she doesn't want to give me any information.

"Listen to me—I'm the woman from the Indian store, the Spice Bazaar," I tell her. "I helped your husband once, a long time ago. Now you must help me."

"All right," the woman says at last, although she is still suspicious. "Haroun has no phone, but I'll tell you how to get to his apartment and when to find him there."

She gives me directions to Haroun's apartment, and tells me how to get there by bus. She also tells me to go early in the morning, before eight o'clock.

"Thank you," I say gratefully. "I'll go there early tomorrow morning."

I walk home, thinking about what I'm going to say to Haroun. I will apologize to him, and warn him that something bad may happen. I will tell him that I want to give him something to protect him.

When I get back to the store, I see a small white note stuck to the door.

I came hoping to see you, but you had gone out. I didn't know that you ever left the store. But now I know that you do, I feel better about asking you this. Will you come to San Francisco with me tomorrow? I want to share with you the places that I love. I'll come early to pick you up, and I'll bring you back before night. Please say yes.

Raven.

"My Raven," I think. And like any woman in love, I press my cheek on the paper where his hand has touched it.

"Yes," I whisper happily. "Tomorrow will be our day of pleasure."

But then other thoughts come.

"What will people think when they see my handsome American with me—an old woman with wrinkled skin? And also, I have nothing pretty to wear."

Then I remember Haroun. I put the paper on which I wrote the directions to Haroun's apartment into a small leather bag. I'll ask Raven to take me there early tomorrow morning.

All evening, I walk backwards and forwards in the store, thinking about how I can make myself look better for Raven. I don't want to look beautiful, just a little younger. I don't care about myself, I want to protect my Raven from people who might laugh at him.

But I do know that I could use the spices to change myself into a beautiful woman. It's difficult not to think about that. I start to go towards the inner room where the rare spices are kept, but I stop myself. I will not use their powers to help myself. If I do that, I will be cursed[3] for all eternity.

10

A Paradise on Earth

Today, the dawn light is soft and golden. I stand in the store waiting for Raven, wearing my old cream-colored sari, aware of the deep wrinkles on my face. I feel sad because I am so ugly. I'm almost wishing that Raven won't come. But when he arrives, he takes my hand in his, and kisses me softly on the cheek.

"Look," he says, opening a package. "I brought you something."

Inside the package is the most beautiful white dress that I have ever seen.

"But I can't wear this, Raven," I say. "It's a dress for a *young* woman."

"No," he says. "It's a dress for a *beautiful* woman."

"How can you say that, Raven?" I ask angrily. I pull him to the window so that he can see my face clearly in the sunlight. "Can't you see that I'm ugly and old? That dress would look ridiculous on me. And you and I together, we will look ridiculous!"

He puts his arms around me and touches my hair. My face presses against his chest. I feel his warm skin under his soft white shirt.

"Tilo," he says. "Please put on the dress. I know that this body isn't the real you. Perhaps I can see you better than you see yourself." He puts the dress in my arms and says. "Please hurry. I want to take you to the ocean today."

So I put on the dress and we go outside and get into Raven's car. It's long and low, and a shiny, dark red color. It moves easily through the traffic, like a great beast of the jungle.

I have asked Raven to take me to Haroun's apartment before we go to the ocean. I climb up the dark stairs to Haroun's door, carrying a packet of *kalo jire* seeds. I call his name and knock on the door until my hands hurt. At last, the door of the apartment opposite Haroun's opens, and a woman's face peers[4] out at me. She is a pretty woman with lovely dark eyes.

"Haroun left a few minutes ago," she says.

I'm really upset that I've missed him this morning. Why did I waste so much time putting on this foolish dress? I sit down in the corridor. I don't want to move. But after a time, I feel Raven's hands on my arms, pulling me up.

"Tilo, you can't wait here all day," he says. "Listen, we'll stop here again on our way home. But now will you do something for me? Be happy, OK? Please! I need you to be happy."

"OK," I say. And suddenly the feeling of weight that was inside me is lifted from me. We walk down the stairs together and drive over the Bay Bridge to San Francisco.

Later, after we have visited Fisherman's Wharf, Twin Peaks, and the Golden Gate Bridge, we stop for our lunch. We sit high on a cliff overlooking the ocean, drinking pale golden wine. Raven has brought a wonderful picnic and we spread the food on the ground. There's a long loaf of bread, some delicious cheeses, and a wooden bowl filled with sweet strawberries.

I watch the waves of the Pacific Ocean crashing onto the shore below us, and listen to the cries of the sea birds in the air above us. I lean back against the trunk of a cypress tree, feeling as elegant as a queen.

"What do you dream about, Raven?" I ask.

"I dream of a paradise on earth," he says shyly. "A place high in the mountains, where the air is filled with the smell of pine trees and eucalyptus trees. A place with a cool, fresh stream. A place where you can be close to Nature. A place where you can live close to bears and antelopes, and watch the birds circling in the wide sky. A place where there are no other people."

Later, Raven continues his story about his mother's family.

"The old man who died on the bed in that dirty house was my great-grandfather—my mother's grandfather. That day, I stood in front of him, and he held out his hands to me. He spoke in a language that I couldn't understand, but the meaning of his words was clear to me. 'Welcome,' he was saying.

"Then a strange thing happened to me. Suddenly, I saw visions of strange people and strange places, and I realized that my great-grandfather was showing me scenes from his life. There was great kindness in his face, and his brown eyes glowed. I knew that he was offering me a choice—to go home with my mother, or to stay in that house and live with his people.

"As soon as I understood this, the old man reached into his shirt and took out a beautiful black bird—a raven. And as he did this, I heard my mother's voice behind me. 'No,' she said harshly.

"I was frightened and I pulled my hand away from the old man. At that moment, the bird flew up into the air and my great-grandfather fell forward in the bed. He had died. As the bird flew away, one black feather fell from its wing into my hand. I looked at the old man's dead body and I felt sick with guilt.

"But my mother was pulling me towards the door. I was angry with her. 'You made me hurt my great-grandfather!' I shouted at her. 'He died because I wouldn't stay with him.' My mother looked into my eyes. 'He was dying anyway,' she said in a calm voice. 'We had nothing to do with his death. I'm only sorry that I brought you here. We're leaving now.' She pulled me out of the house.

"Outside, people were sitting around, eating greasy food from dirty plates. 'Look carefully at these people,' said my mother in a voice full of disgust. 'Don't forget what you've seen here. This is what your life would be like if you did what he wanted.' And then we got into the car and we drove away."

Raven has been talking for a long time. It is now sunset and we watch the sun beginning to sink into the sea.

"Let's go for a walk on the beach," says Raven. "There's just enough time before we have to return."

We walk beside the ocean and he continues his story.

"After that day," he says, "things were never good between my mother and me. I couldn't forgive her for taking me away from my great-grandfather."

"What about your father?" I ask.

"My father knew something was wrong," says Raven, "but I couldn't talk to him about it. He didn't know about my mother's Native American family. And one day, he was killed in an accident at the place where he worked, and my mother and I were left alone. I knew that I should look after her, but I couldn't feel anything for her. I had loved her so much once, but now I just felt a great cold emptiness inside me."

"Oh, Raven," I say. "I'm so sorry." I kiss him softly on the cheek. I feel a great pity for him.

Suddenly he puts his arms around me and kisses me passionately. I've never been kissed like this before, and I can't believe how wonderful it feels.

As we hold each other, I hear the sound of laughter. Two very attractive young girls are walking along the cliff. Their legs are smooth and long and golden-brown, and they have beautiful clothes and hair. They are looking at Raven and me, and they are laughing.

"Some people have very strange tastes[4]," says one of the girls. The other girl laughs again and I see the lovely shape of her neck and her breasts. And then I'm very angry.

"And that dress," says her friend. "Did you see that dress?"

"It's sad, isn't it," says the other one. "Some women will do anything to try to look younger than they are."

They walk on past us. I feel the anger rising up through my body in hot waves. In a moment, I will put a curse on these girls and change their beautiful faces forever.

"Don't listen to them," says Raven, holding me tightly by the arm. "They don't know you, they don't know who you really are. They don't understand about you and me. You mustn't let them spoil the rest of our day."

Raven holds me until the anger has left me.

But the rest of the day *is* spoiled. We go back to the car in silence, and when Raven tries to put his arm around my shoulders, I move away from him.

———

Raven stops the car in front of Haroun's place.

"I'll come to the store tomorrow," he says.

"No, I'll be busy," I tell him.

"The day after tomorrow, then."

"I'll be busy then, too." I don't know why I'm behaving like this.

He takes my hand and kisses my palm. "Dear Tilo," he says, "I'll come then anyway."

I go upstairs to Haroun's apartment, still feeling the warmth of Raven's lips on my hand. Soon, I am almost smiling again.

11

The Red Spice of Anger

I knock at Haroun's door, but nobody answers. I call out his name, and hit the door harder and harder with my hand.

The woman who lives opposite Haroun's apartment opens her door.

"He hasn't returned yet," she says.

She tells me that her name is Hameeda. And she tells me other things about herself. Until a few years ago, she lived in India with her husband. But her husband divorced her because she didn't have any sons, so she came to live with her brother in America.

She has made a new life for herself here.

"Haroun is such a kind neighbor," she says. I notice that whenever she talks about Haroun, her face goes red. I realize that she is in love with him. This is good!

At last we hear footsteps on the stairs. When Haroun comes around the corner of the stairs, I am shocked to see that his face is covered with blood. He has been attacked. He reaches the top of the stairs and falls down in the corridor.

Hameeda runs to fetch a cloth and hot water. We find Haroun's keys and open his door, then carry him into his apartment and lay him on his bed. Hameeda calls a doctor. The doctor soon arrives and gives Haroun an injection of a painkilling drug. Then he stitches his wounds.

"He'll be fine in a few days," the doctor says to us. "Make him rest."

I sit beside Haroun's bed, thinking sadly that I've failed to protect him. And I make a promise to myself. I will not fail again.

When I reach the store, I am so tired that I can hardly open the door. But when I enter, I see that something is lying on the floor inside. It is a small piece of alum[4]. It has a strange, cold glow.

How did the alum get into the store? And why is it here? I move my fingers over its smooth surface, and suddenly I notice something strange. I can feel that the alum has some kind of design carved into it. I look closely at it. With horror, I see the shape of the firebird, Shampati. But Shampati isn't rising from a fire. It's flying *into* one!

"Shampati's Fire is calling me back to the Island," I whisper to myself.

I shut the door and try to concentrate. I know that the Mistress rules say I have only three days left before the Fire takes me back. I have broken too *many* of the rules, and now I must be punished.

Yes, I understand that and I accept it. But first I must think about Haroun. I close my eyes and see a picture of a man attacking him. Again I feel a wave of anger rising inside me. I need to stop all the injustice[4] and violence that happens to innocent Indian people like Haroun in this city.

Kalo jire isn't strong enough to help Haroun now. There is only one spice which is powerful enough, but it is very dangerous to use because it can cause terrible destruction. I go into the inner room and take down a red jar which contains *lanka*—red chillies. I pour the chillies onto a square of white silk, and tie the ends together to make a bundle. Then I begin a powerful chant.

Suddenly, unexpectedly, I have a vision of the Old One's face.

"Tilo, you shouldn't have opened the red jar," she says. "You shouldn't release the *lanka's* angry power into this city—a city that has so much anger already."

But I cannot stop the chant now.

"The power of the chilli is pure. It will cleanse the evil from the city," I say aloud.

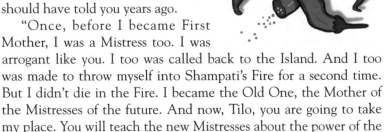

"There isn't much time for us, Tilo," the Old One says. "I'm going to die soon. So let me tell you what I should have told you years ago.

"Once, before I became First Mother, I was a Mistress too. I was arrogant like you. I too was called back to the Island. And I too was made to throw myself into Shampati's Fire for a second time. But I didn't die in the Fire. I became the Old One, the Mother of the Mistresses of the future. And now, Tilo, you are going to take my place. You will teach the new Mistresses about the power of the spices."

I can't see the Old One's face any more, but my mind is full of questions. Is it my destiny to become the new First Mother? Is this what I want?

I notice that the bundle in my hands feels different. It feels heavy. There are no longer chillies inside the cloth. I can feel something else there—something smooth and hard.

I know what the *lanka* has given me for Haroun. A gun.

———

Someone is knocking at my door. I must have been sleeping. It is already late evening. Geeta is standing outside the store, waiting for me to open the door.

"I thought that perhaps I had come on the wrong day," she says. "I was about to leave."

I take her hand, pull her into the store, then into the inner room.

"I'm so glad you didn't leave," I say. "Please stay in here for a short time." I have made a plan, but before I have time to tell her about it, someone else knocks at the door. It's Geeta's father, Ramu. He has come to tell me about *his* father.

"I'm very worried about him," says Ramu. "He's got terrible stomach pains. And he won't let me take him to the hospital. He told me to come here instead. He said that you would be able to help him."

"Yes," I say. "I have something in the inner room. But you must help me find it. It's in a corner. You'll know it when you see it."

I open the door and Ramu goes inside the room where Geeta is waiting. When I hear their cries of surprise, I close the door behind him. I am praying that the spices will work their magic, and solve this family's problems.

I wait by my counter, and at last the door opens again. Ramu approaches me angrily.

"Old woman, you have tried to trick me!" he shouts. "Did you think such a simple trick would work and that I would forgive that ungrateful child so easily?"

I feel a terrible sadness. So my plan hasn't worked!

But suddenly, Ramu starts to laugh. And then Geeta is standing in the doorway and she is laughing too, although her face is wet with tears.

"Please forgive me," Ramu says to me, smiling. "I couldn't resist playing a trick on *you*, in return for the trick that you and my father have played on me."

"Your father's stomach pains are real," I say, giving Ramu a small bottle of medicine. "Give him some of this once every hour, until the pains stop."

They leave the store together, smiling. Ramu has his arm around his daughter's shoulders—the daughter who he has lost and found again.

———

This morning I am very busy. I'm writing signs. BIGGEST SALE OF THE YEAR. BEST BARGAINS IN TOWN. EVERYTHING MUST BE SOLD.

But every now and again I find myself at the window, looking out into the familiar street. I feel a great sadness at the thought that soon I will no longer be here. One idea keeps coming into my mind—what if I refuse to go back to the Island?

I remember the Old One's words.

"If a Mistress is called back and refuses to come, she is brought back anyway. And then all those around her—all those she loves—will be destroyed by Shampati's Fire."

I think of all the people I love in different ways—Raven, the Old One, Haroun, Geeta and her grandfather, Kwesi, Jagjit, and Lalita. I can't risk destroying them.

———

In the middle of the morning, Raven comes into the store and sees the signs I have put up.

"Why are you having a sale?" he asks in surprise.

"Oh, it's just an Indian tradition for the end of the year."

"I came to tell you the rest of my story," he says, "if you have time to hear it."

"This is the best time I'll ever have," I say.

"After my father's death," says Raven, "I had no one to love, and the only thing I was really interested in was power. So I left our home and I went to business school. I was very successful. I had everything I wanted. But money was the only thing I cared about."

"What happened to your mother?" I ask.

"I never saw her again. A couple of years after I left home, I visited my old neighborhood. But a different family was living in our old house. They told me they didn't know what had happened to my mother.

"I needed to tell her that I was sorry for my earlier coldness to her. I wanted us to forgive each other. But it was too late, so I began taking more risks with my life. I took part in dangerous sports and I took drugs. But one day, the drugs made me very ill.

"I was taken to a hospital. The doctors were afraid that I was going to die. That night I had a terrible dream. I was standing on a burning hill in the middle of a lake of fire. I called for help but nobody came. So I threw myself off the top of the hill into the burning lake.

"But as I fell, a huge, beautiful, black raven saved me. It carried me to the place I told you about—a paradise full of trees and cool streams. In my dream, I knew that this was a place where I could grow strong and whole again.

"I'm sure the place is a real place. And I'm sure it's the place where I will find happiness. That's what the bird came to tell me. The day after my dream, I changed my name to the name of the bird that saved me—Raven.

"Recently I've been dreaming about my paradise again. And when I wake up I feel warm, as though sunshine is glowing inside my chest. Do you know when these dreams started again?"

"No," I whisper.

"It was when I met you. And in my latest dreams, you've been there with me, in that perfect place. I want to try and find it." His eyes are dark and beautiful. "Will you come with me, Tilo?"

He leans over the counter and touches my hands.

"Come back tomorrow night," I say. "I'll give you my answer then."

12

The King of Spices

In a box on its own shelf in the inner room is the King of Spices, *makaradwaj*, the spice that can conquer[4] time.

I have made a decision. I do want to be beautiful for Raven, just for one night. I take the box which contains the *makaradwaj*. I can feel it growing warm in my hand.

"Make me beautiful, makaradwaj," I say softly, "so that for just one night, Raven will be dazzled[2], and I will be fixed in his mind forever. I know that I'm wrong to ask this for myself, but I won't pretend that I'm sorry."

If *makaradwaj* is not used properly, it can be very dangerous. It can bring madness, or even death. You have to measure out a tiny quantity and mix it with milk and fruit juice. Then you should drink a small amount of the mixture every few hours, for three days and nights. But I don't have three days and nights before the Fire calls me. So I drink all the mixture now.

Immediately I feel a burning in my throat. It is as if my neck and throat are on fire. The pain reaches all the way down to my stomach.

But suddenly the pain disappears, so that I can breathe again. Then I feel something quite different. Now the *makaradwaj* is beginning to work, and it is as if the bones in my body are growing straighter and stronger. I hear the voice of the spice inside my head.

"By tomorrow night you will be more beautiful than you have ever been," says the voice. "Enjoy your beauty, because the next morning it will be gone."

———

Today I wake up at dawn. The sky is a beautiful pale blue and the air smells of roses. I lie on my hard bed for a while, feeling afraid. At first, I don't want to know how I look. But after a minute, I hold up my hands. The wrinkles on my skin have all disappeared, and my fingers are thin and smooth. I get up and take a shower, slowly moving my hands over my body, which is growing firmer and younger all the time.

But I have a lot of work to do. I pull my hair back from my face and twist it into a knot. I put on my American clothes from the Sears store. Then I open the front door and put up a sign which says: STORE CLOSING FOR EVER—LAST DAY OF SALE.

Soon many people have heard the news and have come to the store, looking for bargains. I sell most of my stock, and soon the drawer of the cash register is full of money. I take the money from the drawer and put it into a paper sack.

"Who are you?" the customers ask over and over again. They don't recognize me because I look so young and so different. So I pretend that I am the old woman's niece, and that she is closing the store because she has become ill.

Late in the afternoon, Geeta's grandfather comes.

"My stomach is still hurting a little," he says as he comes through the door, "but I had to come to thank you, and to tell you what happened."

Then he stops and looks at me carefully.

"Who are you?" he asks.

I tell him, too, that I am the old woman's niece and that my aunt is going away.

"But how can she leave us so suddenly?" he asks. "It's not right. You say she is ill. But she has so many powers, surely she could—"

"She can't use her powers to heal herself," I say quickly. "But tell me, did Geeta return to your house last night?"

"How did you know about that?" he asks in surprise.

"My aunt told me about your problem. She said you might come here today."

He looks at me for a long time. "Yes," he says finally. "She did return. We all sat together and talked. Everyone was very happy and very careful not to talk about things that might cause anger. Then finally Ramu said, 'Well, Geeta, perhaps you should ask your young man to come here for a visit.' And Geeta said, 'If you wish, Dad.' And everyone went to bed, smiling."

"I'm so happy for them," I say. "And for you."

"So your aunt is really not coming back?" he asks.

"I don't think so."

"Your eyes are very like hers," he says, looking carefully at me again. "They are very beautiful. Tell your aunt that I'll say a prayer for her."

"Thank you," I say. "She needs prayers."

After Geeta's grandfather leaves, an attractive, friendly young person that I have never seen before comes to the door. She is the mailwoman and she delivers a letter for me.

I look at the handwriting on the envelope, but I don't recognize it. I lock the door before I open the letter. It is from Ahuja's wife, Lalita.

I'm not living at our house in Oakland any longer. I left my husband a week ago and I'm staying in another city.

Do you remember the magazine you gave me? On the back page were notices. One said, "If you are a battered[4] woman, call this number for help." So the next time my husband beat me, I did call the number. I spoke to a woman who told me she worked for an organization that helps battered women. She was Indian, like me. She was very kind and she said she would help me. I packed a bag and took my passport and some jewelry. The woman came to my house and picked me up. She drove me to this house, in another town.

I don't know what I'll do next. The people here have given me lots of books to read about my rights. They tell me that if I want to file a complaint[4] with the police, they'll help me. Also they can help me to start up a small dressmaking business.

Sometimes I'm afraid, and so sad. Here, I share a room with two other women. I have no place to be alone and there's only one bathroom for six people to share. But I remember what you said to me. I tell myself that I deserve happiness. Please pray that I remain strong enough to find it.

Yours,
> *Lalita.*

I hold the letter tightly and my eyes fill with tears—tears of happiness for Lalita, but also tears of sadness for the wasted years of her life.

I hear a noise in the street, just outside the store. I am worried and I open the door very quietly. A young man is standing on the sidewalk, looking through the window at the poster for Kwesi's One World Dojo. It is Jagjit. I touch his shoulder before he knows that I am there. He turns around quickly.

"Hey, lady, you shouldn't move so quietly," he says angrily. "If you scare people, you might get hurt."

"You scared me too," I say.

He looks at me more closely.

"Wait a minute. You're not the old woman who owns this store."

"No," I say. "I'm her niece. But I know who you are. My aunt told me that you might come. She said that you were a fine young fellow, that you could be anything that you wanted."

"She said that?" For a moment his face has a boyish look of pleasure.

"Do you want to buy something?" I ask.

"No. I was just passing by. I don't even know why I stopped. Maybe it was this poster about the karate school."

"Do you like karate?" I ask.

"I've never tried to learn it. The lessons are much too expensive."

Suddenly I have an idea. Perhaps there is a way to save Jagjit.

"My aunt left something for you," I tell him. "She said it was very important."

I go to the inner room and get the sack of money that the customers spent in my store today. There is more than a thousand dollars there. I write a note to put into the sack. I'm going to give the money to Jagjit, so that he can attend Kwesi's karate school.

When I give the bag to Jagjit, he doesn't understand.

"This is for me?" He reads the note again and again.

For Jagjit, my world conqueror. Start a new life from today. Use the power, but don't let it use you.

"That sounds good to me," I tell him. "My aunt is very wise."

His eyes are shining as he thinks about the future. He thinks of fame and wealth. Perhaps he will become a movie actor, like Bruce Lee. I give him some spices for protection, and he smiles at me.

"Tell your aunt, thanks. Tell her that I'm going to try my best," he says.

Then he disappears into the night. I can only hope and pray for him.

"Jagjit," I whisper, "I hope you will succeed."

13

"I'm Still the Same Tilo"

All the customers have gone. Everything in the store has been sold or given away, except the things that I will need to make Shampati's Fire. But I don't want to think about that now.

I put on the beautiful white dress which Raven gave me. Then I fill a small silk bag with some pieces of lotus root, the spice of love. I tie it on a silk cord and hang it around my neck.

But there is one more thing I want to do. I want to see my reflection in the mirror. This is forbidden, but I have broken so many rules, I don't care about them any more.

I go to the wall where the mirror is hanging and remove its cover. I am completely dazzled by what I see. The face looking back at me is perfect, like the face of a goddess. The only parts of me that I recognize from my past are my eyes. They look wide and frightened.

Now it is night and someone is knocking at the door. I move towards it slowly. My whole body is shaking with desire and fear.

"Tilo," calls Raven from the street. "Open the door, please."

When I open the door and he sees my beauty, he is astonished. I put my hands against his cheeks.

"Raven," I say gently, pulling his arms around me. "Can't you see that I'm still the same Tilo?"

He looks more closely and his arms tighten around me.

"Yes," he says. "I see it in your eyes."

"Then take me with you."

We drive to his apartment. But there is something I have to do on the way there. I am carrying a package containing the gun. I am going to give it to Haroun, so he can defend himself if he is attacked again.

Raven waits in the car as I walk up the stairs to Haroun's apartment. In my head I can hear a voice. Is it mine, or is it First Mother's voice?

"Tilo, are you sure about what you are doing?" asks the voice.

And in fact, I'm not sure at all. I'm afraid that what I'm doing is very wrong.

The door of Haroun's apartment isn't locked. I push it open. It's dark inside. Haroun is lying on the bed, half-asleep.

"Haroun," I whisper. He moves a little. He can't see me in the

darkness but he recognizes my voice.

"Hello, Lady."

"Are you OK? Has the doctor been here?"

"Yes. He is being very kind, and my neighbor, Hameeda, is also being kind. She cooks all my meals and she sits on the bed telling me stories to keep me cheerful." His voice is happy as he talks about Hameeda. He loves her too, and I am glad.

"Haroun, aren't you angry about what happened to you?" I ask him.

"Yes," he replies. "Of course I'm angry." He is silent for a moment. "But I've been lucky. The doctor says I will be all right."

72

"Haroun, I came to say goodbye."

"But where are you going? What will happen to the store?"

"I don't know," I tell him. "But I have something to give you before I go."

"What have you brought me?" asks Haroun curiously.

And suddenly I know what I must give him. Not the gun. Violence is not the answer to Haroun's problems. Instead, I take the silk bag of lotus root from my neck and put it into his hands.

"This is for you and Hameeda," I tell him. "She must wear this bag around her neck on your wedding-night. Then your love for one another will always be passionate."

Haroun doesn't reply, I can tell that he is pleased. I walk towards the door.

"Haroun, please be careful when you return to work," I say.

"Yes, Lady. I won't take any more risks. I won't go into dangerous neighborhoods, or drive customers that I have bad feelings about."

Haroun says goodbye to me. He has so much to live for now.

Downstairs, Raven is waiting impatiently.

"You were gone a long time," he says, a little suspiciously. "Why do you look so happy?"

"Raven!" I say, laughing. "Are you jealous?"

"Of course I'm jealous! You look so beautiful tonight."

He touches my cheek, then pulls me to him and kisses me. "Hey, you still have that package," he says. "I thought that's why you came here—to give it to your friend."

"I changed my mind, Raven. Will you take me to one more place?"

I ask him to take me to the ocean. The package in my hand feels very heavy, but I'm sure I'm doing the right thing. It is better for Haroun to live a life full of love, not hate. I feel the package glowing with heat. And then I hear the voices of the spices in my head—angry voices.

"Tilo, you called us to create a <u>weapon</u> of destruction," the voices say. "Now the destructive power which you have set free will

73

shake the whole city. It will touch every life around you."

But I don't want to listen to these voices. I throw the package into the water and it disappears.

———

Raven lives on the top floor of a very tall building. We go up in an elevator with glass walls, and I feel as if I am flying.

His apartment is simply but richly furnished with soft, white carpets and wide, low sofas of smooth, white leather. The bed cover is made of embroidered white silk. One whole wall of the bedroom is made of glass, so that I can see the tiny yellow lights of the city far below.

Raven turns off the lamp and starts to kiss me. In the silver moonlight I see his strong, beautiful face. His skin smells of almonds and peaches. I have never made love with a man before, and I never thought I would learn about the pleasure of love so fast. But the King of Spices, *makaradwaj*, shows me exactly what to do. Soon, pleasure is flowing through me like warm honey.

———

Afterwards, we lie in each other's arms.

"Tilo, dear one," Raven whispers softly, "I can hardly believe that we'll be together like this forever."

But later, while he is sleeping, I go to his kitchen, where I write a note. Then I go to the bathroom and open a cupboard. I wrap the note around a tube of toothpaste, where Raven will find it in the morning.

I wake him now. I tell him that I must return to the store.

"But why can't we stay together till morning?" he asks.

I think about Shampati's Fire. By dawn the Fire will be burning, and Raven must be far away from me. So I make my voice cold and formal, and I tell him that I need to be alone, to think about my future.

Raven is upset. I know that I have hurt him badly.

"I thought we were going to have no more secrets," he says. "And what about our paradise in the mountains? Aren't we going to search for it together? We mustn't waste any more time, now that we've found each other."

Outside the stars are fading in the sky. In a few hours it will be dawn. I know that I have to hurry.

"OK," I say. "Take me home now and leave me there. But come back in the morning, and I'll go with you." I say this, but I know I won't be there to meet him.

We drive to the store in silence. Raven is still upset with me. We listen to a news reporter on the radio. He is saying that all the animals in the Oakland Zoo have been behaving strangely, crying and calling all night.

I think about Shampati's Fire which is waiting for me. I think about the morning, when Raven will find the note which I left in his bathroom. And I think about what I wrote in the note.

Raven, forgive me. I don't expect you to understand. But you must believe that I have no choice. I do not know where I am going. I do not know whether I shall live or die. But know that I will remember our love forever.
Tilo

14

The Punishment of the Spices

I wait until Raven has driven away before I unlock the door of the store.

I walk between the empty shelves, saying goodbye to them, and trying to remember all my customers. I remember the place where Haroun first asked me to tell him his future, the place where Ahuja's wife admired a sari, the place where Jagjit in his green turban stood shyly behind his mother. But already I'm beginning to forget what these people looked like.

Soon it will be as First Mother said—I will step into Shampati's Fire and wake up on the Island. I will take the Old One's place there. Perhaps my skin will be burned. Perhaps my body will be old and ugly again. I can feel it changing already.

I bring all that is left in the store—spices and some sacks of rice—and make a pile in the center of the room. Over it I sprinkle my name-spice, *til*, to protect me on my journey. I let the white dress fall to the floor. I must take nothing from my life here. I must leave America as naked as I came to it.

Now I am ready. I cover my hands with turmeric and pick up the stone jar that once held the red chillies. There is one chilli left at the bottom. I sit on the pile of rice and spices and I empty my mind. I push out from it all thoughts of everything that I have loved here. I'm surprised when a great wave of peace flows over me. I hold up the single chilli which I have kept, and chant the words: "Come, Shampati, take me now."

I am very afraid. At any moment, I am thinking, the flames will start. But nothing happens. I wait, then say the words again. And again. Louder each time. But still nothing happens. I am crying the words, trying different chants to make the magic begin. But still there is nothing. There is only silence. A deeper silence than I have ever known before.

And finally, in that silence, I understand the punishment that the spices have prepared for me. They have left me here, alone and without my magic powers. For me, there will be no Shampati's Fire. I have been afraid of it for so long, but now I am afraid of my life without it.

I understand everything now. I shall live in this harsh world as an old woman—an old woman without power, without money, without anybody to help me. How can I go to those people I helped and ask them for *their* help? I don't want to see the pity in their eyes.

And most of all, I don't want Raven to see me like this. I see my future life clearly now. I see the dirty streets which will be my home. I'll have to hide from everyone who knows me. I'll have to sleep in doorways. Maybe it will be better to throw myself off a bridge and feel the cold water covering me.

But no! I am terrified and my heart is aching, but I will accept my punishment for as long as I have to—forever if necessary. Love made me break the Mistress rules. If I had to live my life again, I would behave in the same way. I would again leave my store and go out into America to help Geeta. I would give Haroun the lotus root for love, not the gun for hate. And yes, I would make myself as beautiful as a goddess for Raven.

But now I am very tired. I need to sleep, if only for an hour. So I lie down for the last time in the center of this store which is no longer mine.

———

Suddenly I wake up. A voice is calling my name, as if from very far away. I believe that I have been asleep for only a very short time, but I am no longer sure about anything.

"Tilo, Tilo, Tilo," calls the voice.

I get to my feet quickly. But the floor is moving and shaking and there are crashing sounds all around me. The store is cracking into pieces. The walls shake like paper, the ceiling breaks in two. The floor is rising up like a wave so that it is impossible to stay standing. I fall to my knees. Then the ground shakes again. Something flies through the air and hits me on the head. I feel a terrible pain.

A word comes into my mind—earthquake!

15

The Only Paradise

I am lying in a warm, dark place. I try to move my arms and legs, but I can't because my body is wrapped in something soft. I can turn my head a little, but when I move it, the pain makes me cry out.

"Are you awake?" asks a voice. "Are you OK?"

It's Raven's voice. Are we both dead? Did the earthquake kill us all—Haroun and Hameeda, Geeta and her grandfather, Kwesi, Jagjit, Lalita?

But after a moment, I understand that I'm alive. Actually, I'm lying on the back seat of Raven's car, and he is driving.

"Can you sit up?" Raven asks me. "There are some clothes near your head. Can you put them on?"

I move my hands over my body, expecting to feel the wrinkled skin of an old woman. And it's true that my body isn't that of a *young* woman any longer, but it isn't the body of an *old* woman either. What has happened? Why haven't the spices punished me?

A voice in my head gives me the answer.

"You were ready to accept our punishment in your heart. That was enough for us. We didn't need to punish your body too."

I put on the clothes—a pair of Raven's jeans and a shirt.

"If you feel OK," says Raven, "come up here beside me."

I move carefully into the front seat. It's dark inside the car. And the city seems darker than I have ever seen it. Then I notice that most of the streetlights we are passing have been broken.

"Tell me what happened," I say.

"After I left you at the store earlier," says Raven, "I started packing for the trip to paradise. I couldn't sleep because I was angry with you. But even when I was angry, I couldn't imagine my future without you."

His words flow over me like sweet wine, warming me. But as I listen, I am looking at the car's mirror. I turn it towards me.

"I need to look at myself," I say. My voice is shaking.

Raven nods his head. I look in the mirror and I see a different woman—a woman who isn't particularly pretty or ugly, a woman who isn't particularly young or old. Just an ordinary woman.

"You know," he says, "this is how I've always thought you should look." Gently, he touches my cheek with his fingers.

"You don't care that my beauty has gone?"

"No. To be honest, I was a bit scared of it last night."

I look in the mirror again, and now I see that my eyes are the same—bright with intelligence, the eyes of someone who is ready to question and to fight.

"Did you read my note?" I ask Raven.

"Yes. I found it when I was packing my bags. You wrote that you were leaving, but didn't know where you were going. That scared me. I had to come and find you before you disappeared.

"I drove towards the store. But, when I was a couple of miles away, the earthquake began. Big cracks opened in the streets and buildings were on fire everywhere. I could hear people screaming and sirens wailing. For a while I was afraid I wouldn't be able to get to you.

"At last I reached the store. But as I got there the walls started to fall. I called your name and began to look for you. At last I saw your hand, and I found you under a pile of bricks.

"Your body had already started to change. I carried you into the car, then I started to drive north. We've been driving for about an hour. We're almost at the Richmond Bridge. It's the only bridge that hasn't been destroyed. We can cross it and keep going north—till we find our paradise."

Raven waits for an answer, but I don't say anything.

"There's a box of roadmaps near your feet," says Raven. "They show different routes into the mountains in the north. Why don't you look through them and choose the route you like best?"

"Me? But I don't know anything about these roads."

"I trust your feelings about things. And if we choose the wrong route, we'll just try another one. We'll just keep searching until we find our paradise." He laughs.

So I choose a map. We're almost at the toll booth[4] of the Richmond Bridge. Raven slows down to pay the toll.

"Where have you come from?" the man in the booth asks. "Oakland? People say that's where the center of the earthquake was."

The car moves forwards over the bridge. I gaze north across the dark water whose surface reflects the stars above us. Beyond the water are the mountains, and somewhere up there will be Raven's paradise. In his mind, it already exists, but can it ever exist for me?

When we reach the other side of the bridge, I put my hand on his arm.

"Stop, Raven."

I can see that he's worried about me. He doesn't know what I might do and, after last night, doesn't really trust me. But he drives into the viewing area[4], where we can look back across the water, and he stops the car. I push open the door and get out. I look towards the south and see the dirty red glow of the burning city across the bay. I have a vision of houses breaking open, of fire engines and police cars in the cracked streets, of people crying out in pain.

"Raven," I whisper. "This is all my fault. I made the earthquake happen."

"Don't be crazy, Tilo," he says. "This is an earthquake zone. Earthquakes happen here every few years." He puts his hand on my arm and tries to guide me back to the car. He cannot understand why I am being so foolish.

But I am remembering the terrible destruction of my village in India, when the pirates came. Tonight, the smell of the burning buildings reminds me of it. That destruction was my fault, and *this* is my fault too. When I threw the package with the gun into the water, I tried to stop the terrible destruction which I had called from the spices. But I was too late to stop it. The powerful forces of destruction were already working.

It would be so easy to turn my back[2] on the burning city across the bay. But I won't do that.

"I can't go with you, Raven."

His eyes are full of pain. "What do you mean?" he says.

"I have to go back to Oakland. I have to try to help the people there. You go on. Please. You don't have to take me back."

"You made a promise to me, Tilo."

"We couldn't be together, Raven," I say sadly, "even if we found your special place. Because there is no paradise—not the kind of paradise *you* are looking for. The only paradise on earth is the one we make for ourselves in the ordinary places where we have to live."

He closes his eyes. I turn to start walking back over the bridge.

"Wait," he says suddenly. "I guess I'll have to come too." He nods his head. "That's right. You heard me."

"Are you sure?" I have to ask him. "It'll be difficult. I don't want you to be sorry that you came with me."

He laughs. "No, I'm not sure at all. I'll probably be sorry about it a hundred times, even before we get back to Oakland."

I hold him tightly in my arms and we kiss for a long time.

"You must help me choose a new name," I say. "My Tilo-life is over. I want a name that belongs to my land and to your land, to India and to America. I belong to both lands now. Is there such a name?"

"What about Maya?"

Maya. Yes, I like the sound and shape of it, the way it feels to say it. It feels cool and wide on my tongue. How different this name-giving is from the last time, when I was given the name of Tilo. Now there are no sister-Mistresses around me, no First Mother to name me. And yet this name is as real as Tilo was. I feel a great happiness.

"Come on," I say to Raven, and holding hands, we walk back towards the car.

Points for Understanding

1

1 The storyteller says that she felt a terrible guilt about the destruction of her village. Why does she think that this was her fault?
2 Something happens in this chapter which tells us that the Old One knows what the storyteller is thinking. What happpens?

2

1 The Old One tells the girls about their future lives. All the girls look down at the ground but the prettiest girls look at the ground the longest. Why do you think this happens?
2 The Old One tells the storyteller about Tilottama. One reason for this is that Tilottama is the name the storyteller has chosen. Give another reason.
3 What can you learn about Oakland from the pictures that Tilo sees in the mist?

3

1 How does Tilo know that Ahuja beats his wife?
2 Why does Tilo want to give Haroun some *kalo jire*?
3 Jagjit's mother asks him if there is something wrong with his eyes. Why? Does she really want an answer? What kind of language is she using?

4

1 Tilo guesses that one of her American customers is lonely. What else do you think she guesses about him? What would be the reason for her guess?
2 Why does Tilo think that she should give asafetida to the lonely American?
3 On the Island, Tilo had told the Old One, "Mother, you don't have to worry about me." Is this still true? Give a reason for your answer.

5

1 "Ramu is my son, but sometimes I don't understand him," Geeta's grandfather tells Tilo. Why does he say this?
2 Geeta's grandfather wants Tilo to visit his granddaughter. Tilo replies, "It isn't permitted." What does she mean?
3 Why do you think Tilo has her terrible dream about the Island?

6

1 "How did the fennel get there?" Tilo asks herself. Why do *you* think the fennel is on top of the magazines? Give a reason for your answer.
2 Kwesi smiles and says, "I'll find another place for the poster." Why?
3 Why do you think Tilo is frightened when she reads in Jagjit's mind that the older boys sometimes ask him to keep a parcel in his locker?

7

1 Geeta's voice is full of hope when she asks Tilo if she has been sent by Ramu. Why do you think this is?
2 Geeta tries to hide her smile, but Tilo knows that she is pleased. What does this tell you about Geeta? Mention two things.

8

1 Who is Evvie?
2 Who is the old man in the bed?

9

1 How does Kwesi want to help young people to protect themselves?
2 Why does Tilo give Geeta's grandfather a medicine that will give him stomach pains?
3 Why does Tilo want to apologize to Haroun?
4 Tilo wants to warn Haroun that something bad might happen. Why does she think this?

10

1 Tilo has bad feelings about the white dress for two reasons. What are they?
2 "Some people have very strange tastes," says a girl on the beach. What does she mean?

11

1 "The city has so much anger already," the Old One tells Tilo in her vision. What does she mean?
2 "I couldn't resist playing a trick on you," Ramu tells Tilo. What trick has he played on her?

12

1 Why does Tilo pretend to be her own niece?
2 Explain what Tilo means in her note to Jagjit.

13

1 Tilo gives Haroun something which she was going to keep for herself. What is this thing? Why does she change her mind about keeping it?
2 What do we learn in this chapter about Raven's plans for the future?

14

1 Why does Tilo keep one red chilli?
2 When you read the last sentence of this chapter, it might remind you of a sentence in Chapter 13. Which sentence is this?

15

1 "Your body had already started to change," Raven tells Tilo. What does he mean?
2 Raven and Tilo have different ideas about paradise. Explain the difference.

Glossary

Terms to do with life and customs in India

Descriptions of Indian spices and how they are used in Indian cooking, and as medicines, are given in the *Note About This Story* on page 6.

buffalo (page 10)
> a large, very strong animal like a cow. Here, the *buffalo* is used by the village water-carrier, whose job is to bring large containers of water from a well to the village.

Diwali (page 27)
> an important festival for members of the Hindu religion. The festival takes place in October or November of each year.

dowry (page 10)
> in some societies, if a girl gets married her parents are expected to give money or property to her husband at the time of the marriage. This gift is the girl's *dowry*.

pakoras (page 24)
> small balls of chopped meat or vegetables which are covered with flour and egg, then cooked in hot oil.

papads—*sabu papads* (page 22)
> circles of thin, crispy bread made from flour, salt, water, and spices. *Papads* are sometimes called *poppadoms*.

sari (page 20)
> a very long, wide piece of cloth which Indian women wrap around their bodies to make a kind of dress.

snacks—*spice snacks* (page 45)
> snacks are small pieces of food which are eaten between meals. *Spice snacks* are made from nuts, seeds, etc. and include spices to give them a strong flavor.

turban (page 22)
> a long piece of cloth which some Indian men wrap around the upper parts of the heads, to cover their long hair. *Turbans* are often worn for religious reasons, e.g. by members of the Hindu, Muslim, and Sikh religions.

Some of these terms are metaphors. If you say that something is *like* something else, you are using a simile—e.g. "my friend is like a perfect jewel." If you say that something *is* something else, you are using a metaphor—e.g. "my friend is a perfect jewel." You are speaking metaphorically if you use language which would normally describe one thing (the literal meaning of the words) to describe a different thing—e.g. "a wave of anger rushed through my body."

against—*turned my parents against me* (page 42)
> if you say or do something which makes someone dislike you, you have *turned that person against you.* You can also turn people against someone else by saying bad things about that person.

antidote (page 8)
> the literal meaning of an *antidote* is a medicine that stops the effects of a drug or a poison. Here, it means a medicine to stop someone falling in love.

arrogant (page 14)
> if you are rude or unpleasant to someone because you think you are better than he or she is, your behavior is *arrogant.* Arrogant people are often impatient—they don't wait to hear what other people have to say.

back—*turn my back on* (page 82)
> if you know that someone has a problem, but you decide to ignore it and do nothing about it, you are *turning your back on* that person. You can also turn your back on a problem.

dazzled (page 66)
> the literal meaning of to *dazzle someone* is to make him unable to see properly by shining a very bright light in his eyes. But it is also used metaphorically, when it means to make someone astonished at the great beauty, or skill, or intelligence of someone or something.

door—*the door of my mind* (page 24)
> Tilo can often tell what thoughts are in people's minds. She uses the metaphor of a door which leads to someone's mind, and which can be open or closed, to describe whether or not it is possible to tell what the person is thinking. Here she is talking about the door to her own mind, which she keeps closed. This is because she does not want Kwesi to know what she is thinking.

feelings—*hurt his feelings* (page 36)

if you say something which makes someone unhappy, you have *hurt that person's feelings*.

guilt (page 12)

if you have done something wrong and you feel bad about it, you are feeling *guilt*.

heart—*my heart fills with sorrow* (page 23)

people often talk metaphorically about their hearts when they really mean their feelings. They say that their hearts *fill with*, or *are full of*, one emotion or another. Here Tilo means that she felt very sad about Jagjit's problems.

longed—*longed for* (page 11)

if you want something very badly, you *long for* that thing. This feeling is called a *longing*.

vain (page 11)

if you are very pleased with something about yourself—usually the way you look—you are *vain*.

wave—*a wave of joy rushing through me* (page 16)

See the note at the beginning of this section. In this book, emotions are often described as flowing through, or over, Tilo. Here, a wave of the sea is used as a metaphor for the feeling of joy which comes quickly and suddenly to Tilo.

SECTION 3

Terms to do with magic and unusual powers

caul (page 10)

sometimes children are born with a piece of thin, loose skin covering their heads and shoulders. This is called a *caul*. In some countries this is a sign of good luck, in others it is a sign of bad luck.

chanting (page 15)

a *chant* is a simple kind of song which uses the rhythm of speech and does not have many different notes. Chants often form part of a religious ceremony. If you sing in this way, you are *chanting*.

cursed—*cursed for all eternity* (page 54)

if you are *cursed*, someone has used magic powers to make life bad for you. *Eternity* means all time, without an end.

destiny (page 12)

something which is going to happen to you in the future, and which you can't escape, is your *destiny*. If you accept that this will happen, you are *following your destiny*.

foretold (page 10)

    if you know that something unexpected is going to happen before it does happen, and you tell someone about it, you have *foretold* that thing.

fortune—*tell my fortune* (page 21)

    if you tell someone the events of his or her future life, you are *telling that person's fortune*. His or her fortune is everything that is going to happen to him or her. Some people try to tell other people's fortunes by looking at the lines on the palms of their hands. If you do this to someone, you are *reading his or her palm*.

healing—*words of healing* (page 21)

    to *heal* somebody who is sick means to make them well, to cure them. In magic or religious ceremonies, magicians and priests try to heal people simply by speaking special words—*words of healing*.

spirit—*traveling in the spirit* (page 44)

    some people believe that your mind, or your spirit, can leave your body when you are asleep and travel to other places. Later your spirit returns to your body. When your mind leaves your body behind like this, you are *traveling in the spirit*.

vows (page 15)

    very serious promises about the future, which often have to do with religion.

SECTION 4
General

alum (page 61)

    a chemical. This piece of *alum* looks like a lump of salt and has a picture carved on it.

area—*viewing area* (page 81)

    a piece of land next to a road where you can stop your car to admire the view of the surrounding places.

battered (page 68)

    to *batter* someone means to beat and injure them. Women whose husbands are violent towards them are often called *battered wives* or *battered women*.

billion (page 6)

    a thousand millions.

bin (page 26)

    a large container.

booth—*toll booth* (page 81)

sometimes you have to pay to drive your car across a bridge or along a piece of road. These bridges and roads are called toll bridges and toll roads. The toll is the amount that you have to pay to use them. You pay this toll at a toll booth.

bows (page 36)

when you *bow,* you bend the upper part of your body forward. This is a formal greeting which people can make when they meet, or part from, someone.

bully (page 23)

if a strong person attacks a younger or weaker person without a reason, the strong person *bullies* the weaker person, and he or she can be described as a *bully.*

Chicano (page 31)

a male citizen of the United States who was born in Mexico, or whose family was originally from Mexico.

cleaner—*Vaccuum Cleaner Repair Store* (page 19)

a *vacuum cleaner* is an electric machine which sucks in dirt and dust from floors and other surfaces. This repair store is where people take broken cleaners to be mended. The store also repairs *sewing machines*—machines for stitching pieces of cloth together.

complaint—*file a complaint* (page 69)

if somebody commits a crime and you tell the police about it, you are *filing a complaint* with the police about that person.

conquer (page 66)

if you win a battle against someone or something, you *conquer* that person or thing. You are the *conqueror* of that person or thing.

cool (page 38)

a slang word meaning "good" or "OK."

counter (page 20)

a large, low cupboard in a store. It often has a glass front and sometimes a glass top, so that goods can be displayed inside it. The people who work in the store usually stand behind a counter to serve their customers.

destroyed (page 12)

when something is *destroyed,* it is broken and damaged so badly that it cannot be repaired. When something is destroyed, the action is called the *destruction* of the thing.

dojo (page 37)

a school where you learn fighting skills, e.g. karate. At a "one world" dojo, you can learn fighting skills—martial arts—from several different countries.

down—*beating down* (page 35)

when the sun is shining on a place and it feels very hot, you can say that the sun is *beating down* on that place.

elevator (page 41)

a machine like a small room which moves people from one floor to another in a tall building.

embroidery (page 20)

patterns which are stitched in a piece of cloth, using colored threads. The art of making these patterns is also called *embroidery*, and the patterns are said to be *embroidered* on the cloth.

faded (page 19)

when the color disappears from something because it is old, or it has been in bright sunlight, it *fades*. The thing can be described as *faded*.

formal (page 26)

if you behave or speak in a correct and serious way—a way which is neither friendly nor unfriendly—you are being *formal*.

fragrance (page 15)

a pleasant smell. Something with a smell like this is said to be *fragrant*.

garbage—*weeds and garbage* (page 49)

weeds are plants which are growing where nobody wants them to grow. They are not the kind of plants which people grow because they are beautiful. *Garbage* is something which has been thrown away because its owner no longer wants it, or because it is broken.

hasty (page 51)

if you do something quickly, without thinking about what might happen next, you are being *hasty*.

horizon (page 12)

the line in the distance where the sky seems to meet the sea.

immigrants—*illegal immigrants* (page 31)

an *immigrant* is someone who has left a country to live in another country. If this person enters the country where he wants to live without permission from its government, he is an *illegal immigrant*.

injustice (page 62)

if someone is not treated fairly, and that person's rights are ignored, that is an *injustice*. And if someone commits a crime and that person is not punished for it, that too is an *injustice*.

kidnap (page 11)

if you *kidnap* someone, you take them away from their home and family without their permission.

locker (page 39)

a kind of cupboard at your school or place of work, in which you can lock things to keep them safe.

midwife (page 10)

a nurse who takes care of a woman who is having a baby.

neighborhood (page 36)

a small area of a town or city.

paradise (page 16)

a place that is perfect, where everything is good and nothing is wrong.

passionate (page 8)

showing very strong emotions or feelings.

peers (page 55)

when you *peer* you look carefully at something, especially if it is difficult to see it.

personal (page 46)

something which is private to you, and should not interest anyone else unless you want it to, is *personal* to you—it is your private business. If you talk about things which are another person's private business, you are *being personal*.

pirates (page 11)

robbers who travel on ships. They attack other ships to steal things from them and they also attack people who live near the shores of the sea.

rarest (page 20)

an adjective which means something is least often found, or hardest to find.

register—*cash register* (page 27)

a machine which records or *registers* the money, or *cash*, which a storekeeper takes from his customers for each sale. The machine contains a drawer for keeping the cash in.

resolutely (page 40)

if you do something *resolutely*, you have decided to do that thing after thinking carefully about it, and you will not let anyone stop you.

rest room—*public rest room* (page 40)

a *rest room* is a place where you can wash and use a lavatory. A *public rest room* is one which can be used by anybody.

scholarship (page 42)

you have to pay fees to attend some schools and colleges. If you cannot pay these fees, you can take an exam to win a *scholarship* for the school or college. Each year a small number of people are given these scholarships, and they can attend the school without paying the fees.

shawl (page 12)

a large piece of cloth that a woman wears around her shoulders or over her head.

shrugs (page 37)

he lifts his shoulders and lets them fall again quickly. *Shrugging* is a way of using your body to say, "I don't care" or "I don't know."

shyly (page 49)

if you are *shy*, you are nervous of other people who you do not know well. If you behave *shyly*, you are nervous or embarrassed about talking to, or sharing your thoughts with, other people.

stock (page 26)

all the things which are for sale in a store.

suspiciously (page 35)

if you think that someone has done, or is going to do something wrong, but you don't know this for certain, you are *suspicious* of that person. If you look at someone *suspiciously*, you believe that person has just done, or is going to do something wrong. But if someone is *behaving suspiciously*, that means you are suspicious of the person, not that the person is suspicious of anyone else.

talent (page 20)

if you are good at doing something, you have a talent for that thing.

tastes (page 58)

the types of thing that you like are your *tastes*.

temptations—*to resist the temptations of something* (page 28)

if you want to do something, or want to have something very much, you are being *tempted* by that thing. When this happens, it is called *temptation*. If you try very hard not to want or have things, you are *resisting the temptations* of those things.

though—*as though* (page 17)

if something happens, and you want to compare this with something different happening, you can use the words *as though*, or *as if*. If something is not true, but you feel the same as if it were true, you can use *as if*, or *as though*, e.g. "I feel as if I am twenty years old again."

trees—*eucalyptus trees* (page 16)

tall trees that grow in hot countries. They produce a strongly smelling oil which is used in medicines.

tropical (page 26)

the area around the middle of the earth is called the *tropics*. The tropics are the hottest part of the world, and the weather there is called *tropical*. In the tropics the days end quickly and the nights are very dark.

up—*bringing up* (page 30)

to *bring someone up* means to look after that person from the time when he or she is a child. It also means to teach him or her the *values* which you believe in.

up—*lock up* (page 26)

when you close and lock the doors of a store at the end of the day, or when you close and lock the doors and windows of your house, you are *locking up*. This phrasal verb is not normally followed by an object.

up—*mixed up with* (page 39)

if you spend a lot of time with the same people you are *mixed up with* them.

values—*traditional values* (page 29)

your *values* are your beliefs about the things in life which you think are important, e.g. *religious values* or *family values*. If you have the same values that most people in your country or society have believed in for a long time, these are *traditional values*.

volcano (page 13)

a mountain which has a large hole in its top. From time to time, hot rocks, gas, and ash are forced out of the hole by pressure deep in the Earth. When this happens, the volcano is *erupting*.

wail (page 26)

a high sound which goes up and down regularly. Here the sound is made by *sirens*—machines which are attached to police cars, fire engines, and ambulances, to warn other drivers to get out of their way.

warned (page 15)

if you tell someone very seriously that he or she must not do something, you are *warning* him or her not to do it, and he or she has been *warned* not to do it. Your words are a *warning*.

wrinkles (page 21)

lines in the skin, especially of your face and hands, which appear as you get older. If you have these lines, your skin can be described as *wrinkled*.

Published by Macmillan Heinemann ELT
Between Towns Road, Oxford OX4 3PP
Macmillan Heinemann ELT is an imprint of
Macmillan Publishers Limited
Companies and representatives throughout the world
Heinemann is a registered trademark of Harcourt Education, used under licence.

ISBN 1–405–07327–6
EAN 978–1–405073–27–1

The Mistress of Spices © Chitra Banerjee Divakaruni 1997
First published by Doubleday 1997

This retold version by Anne Collins for Macmillan Readers
First published 2003
Text © Macmillan Publishers Limited 2003
Design and illustration © Macmillan Publishers Limited 2003

This edition first published 2005

Designed by Sarah Nicolson
Illustrated by Shane McGowan
Cover photograph by Stone/Getty Images

Printed in Thailand

2009 2008 2007 2006 2005
10 9 8 7 6 5 4 3 2